Fast Car

Praise for Martina Murphy's Livewire

Fast Car

Martina Murphy

POOLBEG

Published 1998 by
Poolbeg Press Ltd,
123 Baldoyle Industrial Estate,
Dublin 13, Ireland

© Martina Murphy 1998

The moral right of the author has been asserted.

The Arts Council
An Chomhairle Ealaíon

A catalogue record for this book is available from the British Library.

ISBN 1 85371 848 3

Cover illustration by Leonard O'Grady
Cover design by Poolbeg Group Services Ltd
Set by Poolbeg Group Services Ltd in Times 11/13
Printed and bound in Great Britain by
Cox & Wyman Ltd, Reading, Berkshire.

Acknowledgements

Everyone I mentioned the last time around plus:

Colm, my husband, for his support and footballing knowledge.

Claire, my sister, for helping me edit the first shaky drafts of this book (again).

Nicole Jussek for her brilliant editing and all the staff in Poolbeg for their help and encouragement.

Every single person who was at the *brilliant* bash in the Coach House last September (you know who you are). Thanks for your support and help.

To all the members of the media who answered my begging letter and phone calls!

And finally, Liam Harnett, Tom O'Dea, Brendan Tallon, Aisling Corcoran and everyone else who championed the cause of *Livewire*!!

About the Author

Born in 1968, Martina Murphy's passion for writing started early. She began writing her first novel, *Livewire* when she was just fifteen. It was published in 1997 by Poolbeg. *Fast Car* is her second novel. Martina is married with one young son and lives in County Kildare.

To Mam and Dad – with love

Prologue

"April, come here a moment, will you?"

April jumped.

"April, we've something to tell you."

And so they told her.

Her dad not looking once at her and her mother fiddling with her wedding ring and nodding every so often, they told her that her father had been offered a position in Germany for nine months and that she, April, was to be sent to a cousin of her dad's in Dublin to be looked after. They said that they were sorry that they couldn't get someone in Cork to take her. There was no one available.

April cringed when she heard that.

Her dad told her that there was no point in interfering in her education for the sake of nine months. They told her she would like Dublin. They told her that Jim Walsh and his family were really nice. They told her everything. They always told her everything. They were great the way they did that. They told her it was all right to feel sad, only April didn't feel sad. April nodded and agreed with them, but she couldn't make herself feel sad.

She could only feel angry and maybe slightly relieved, but she didn't feel sad and she didn't know why.

Chapter One

"OLÉ! OLÉ!" Jack yelled as he pulled his twin sister, Sarah, into the kitchen. They were both laughing and Sarah, running up to their mother, caught her by the waist and began to swing her around.

"You won, so," Mrs Walsh disengaged herself from her daughter's exuberant embrace. She grinned. "About time, too."

"Flippin' three-nil," Jack said as he took a can of Coke from the fridge. "The first game we've won all season and it was against the league leaders an' all. Imagine, we knocked them out of the first round of the cup!" He began to gulp down his drink then, wiping his mouth with his sleeve and ignoring the look his ma gave, he continued, "It's just as well Luke is back. He scored two and set up the third."

"Yeah, pity it had to be that fecker," Sarah agreed as she rummaged in the press for some biscuits. "But he was brill, Ma. He didn't train or anything. He broke his arm, was off for a few months an' back he comes and it's like he was never away." There were no biscuits so she began to munch on some crackers. "The guy is unbelievable," she said, her mouth full.

"Dinner will be ready soon, so don't eat – right?" Mrs Walsh took the crackers from her.

"Well, how come you let him drink a can, then?"

"I *have* just played a football game, you know," Jack sneered at his sister, his eyes dancing.

"Oh really," Sarah sneered back. "Is that what it was? I thought you were a sub let loose on the pitch by mistake! In fact, I thought that. . ."

Jack picked up the cushion from the kitchen chair and fired it at Sarah, hitting her in the face.

"Ma!" Sarah implored. "Look what he did!"

Mrs Walsh ignored her. They were always bickering, she was not getting involved.

"Huh, if I did that you'd kill me," Sarah's voice had risen a pitch. "You don't say a word to him."

"That's 'cause she loves me the best."

"Oh, for God's sake, will you both shut up," Mrs Walsh snapped. "I'm sick of these constant rows."

"OOOOOH."

"Oh, oh, you said shut up, Ma."

"Ooey, ooey, ooey."

They both cracked up laughing.

She tried not to smile back. God, they drove her mad. One was as bad as the other. Vaguely she wondered how on earth they'd get on with April Gavin, who was due to arrive next week.

"It could calm them down," her husband had said hopefully. "She's just what they need, a nice, studious, brainy girl." Then, as an afterthought, "Maybe Jack'll take a leaf out of her book, huh?" They looked at each other.

"Yeah, well, maybe not," he shrugged.

"Nice thought, though – you've a good imagination, Dan."

They laughed.

4

Chapter Two

The football game over, Luke sat alone in the dressing-room. Jack Walsh had offered him a lift home, but he had refused. The other lads had all gone for a drink to celebrate the win. Luke had told them he would be down later. The silence was comforting and Luke savoured it as he put his football boots into his sports bag. He gazed around at the painted walls and the rotting benches and breathed in the smell of stale sweat. It was good to be back. It was good to be playing football again – the only game that meant anything to him – doing the only thing he knew he was good at. He rubbed his arm, which had begun to ache slightly, and then, hoisting his bag over his shoulder, he began to walk slowly toward the door.

"Luke?" It was Bill, the trainer.

Luke sighed. Now what did he want? "Yeah."

Bill opened the door and grinned at his star player. "Janey, you took your time. I thought we had missed you." He thumbed to another man behind him. "This is John Waters." He said it as if Luke should know him.

Luke nodded. "How you doin'?"

John Waters stuck out his hand, grinning, and said, "Great game. You're a great player."

Luke shrugged and shook the man's hand. "Thanks," he mumbled.

Bill sat down on a seat, oblivious to the fact that it was about to give way. "John here is a friend of mine," he announced importantly. "He's looking for players for Bohs."

John nodded his affirmation.

Luke looked impassive. He ran his hand through his hair and shrugged. "So?"

John laughed. "Well, I was wondering if you would be interested in coming for a trial for the team?"

Luke gulped. His heart began to hammer and, eyes down, he muttered, "Naw, not really."

Both men found it hard to conceal their surprise. Bill jumped up from the bench and grabbed Luke by the shoulders. "Luke – are you mad?" he said. "Just listen to him."

John gulped. Most young lads would jump at the offer. "It's just a trial. It won't happen until the summer at least and you won't have to play for us until you leave school."

"I've already left school," Luke replied. "I left two years ago – after me Junior Cert." He gazed at the two men. "I really got to go now."

"You're a great player," John repeated as he shoved a card into Luke's hands. "You could go anywhere – Bohs would just be a start for you."

Luke said nothing. Bill was gratified to see him pocket the card; at least he didn't throw it away.

"Give us a ring if you change your mind," John said as he left. "We'll arrange a trial date to suit you." He nodded his thanks to Bill and left.

"Are you crazy?" Bill almost yelled. "God, Luke, are you mad?"

"Naw, I'm not mad," Luke shrugged. "I'm just not interested – OK, Bill?"

"You could at least give it a try. You could really make a go of things." He had him by the shoulders again.

Luke glared pointedly at Bill's hands until Bill slowly released him. "I'm happy enough the way things are," he said quietly. "I like playin' for Ballinteer." He left the dressing-room and winced as Bill yelled after him, "ARE YOU HAPPY, LUKE? ARE YOU REALLY? YOU DON'T LOOK TOO HAPPY TO ME!"

Chapter Three

"We've news for you," Mr Walsh looked at his two kids and smiled. They stared back. Sarah looked curious. Jack, well, Jack looked unruffled, as usual, his father thought. "We decided to wait till now to tell you."

"So, what is it?" Jack asked as he shovelled food into his mouth.

"For God's sake, will you eat like a human being," Mrs Walsh chided.

"I am eatin' like a human being," Jack grinned, "a flippin' hungry human being."

Sarah giggled and Mr Walsh sighed in exasperation. The lad would drive you crazy, he thought.

"So what's the news, Pop?" Sarah asked.

Dan Walsh hated when she called him that. He knew she got it from that Frank fella she went out with. 'Frank the Plank', Jack called him. Good name, Mr Walsh thought.

"We're having a visitor for the next nine months or so. A distant cousin of mine, Jim Gavin, has to go abroad and so we're having his daughter to stay."

"Isn't she the swotty one that came on a visit years ago?" Jack asked.

"She's a hard worker," Mr Walsh stared his son down.

"She sounds borin' from what I've heard about her," Sarah mused.

"When's she comin'?" Jack asked.

"Next Saturday. Her father has a work contract in Germany for a while. He wants her to stay here so as not to miss school. She'll be transferring from Cork to here."

"Yeah?"

"It's 'yes', not 'yeah'," Mrs Walsh corrected her daughter.

"Yeah, Ma, I know," Sarah giggled and Jack laughed. The two grinned at each other.

"Don't be cheeky," Mr Walsh snapped.

Sarah swiftly brought the conversation back on track; the last thing she needed was her da in bad humour. "Why can't she stay with someone in Cork?" she asked. "It's a hassle comin' all the way up."

Mr Walsh nodded. "It sure is," he agreed. "But none of their friends in Cork had room for an extra body, so as a last resort Jim asked us to take her. We said fine."

"Huh, some friends," Jack mused.

"It's great, all the same," Sarah was delighted. "Borin' or not – you'll be outnumbered, Jack. She'll be able to back me up when you try and annoy me!" She looked in triumph at her brother. If she had expected him to look worried, she was disappointed.

"Big wow," he made a face. "I'm so scared, Sarah." Then, turning to his father, he asked, "She good-lookin', Da?"

Mr Walsh didn't know how he had expected his offspring to react but it certainly wasn't what he would have wished. His son looking at it as a opportunity to enhance his love life, and his daughter delighted to have a comrade in arms. Mr Walsh sighed and looked glumly

9

at his wife. "We were kind of hoping for a more supportive response from both of you," she said gently. "You'll both have to help her settle in and do your best to show her around, all those kinds of things."

Jack nodded gravely. "Yeah, she'll be another supporter for Ballinteer United, anyhow." He turned to Sarah and said, "You better get yer knittin' needles out, Sis, and knit April a scarf."

Sarah belted him in the arm. "Feck off with your chauvinist comments. You knit her a scarf, why don't you?"

"SARAH!" both her parents cried.

Chapter Four

April lay awake, hands behind her head, staring at the ceiling. This was her first night with the Walshes and she couldn't sleep. She always found it hard to sleep in new places, though, she thought ruefully, she should be well used to it at this stage.

She was also afraid she'd have nightmares – she'd feel stupid if she woke everyone by yelling in her sleep on her first night here.

The room seemed so much brighter than her own at home. She could make out the shapes of the huge posters that adorned the walls. Sarah was a mega Oasis fan, judging by the stuff in this room. She had Oasis scarves and pennants everywhere.

April's own bedroom at home was a sterile affair by comparison.

She bit her lip and concentrated on the room she was now in. Sarah was snoring lightly in the bed across from her and she began to move as if she could somehow sense April studying her. April liked Sarah. She was really chatty and friendly and had so much confidence. She even had a boyfriend, though that wasn't surprising, Sarah was beautiful, April thought. Tall, dark-haired, dark-eyed and with a figure to die for, April had decided that with those looks, Frank, Sarah's fella, was probably even nicer-looking than Brad Pitt. Probably even nicer than two Brad Pitts.

She grinned to herself and, closing her eyes, found her mind wandering back to her arrival that day in Walshes.

Her parents had dropped her off at teatime on their way to the airport. Her dad had struggled to haul her cases up the driveway. Her mother had tottered her way up the path on her high black stiletto heels, and she, April, had clumped along behind them. She must have looked a sight, she thought, in her brown cords and cream blouse, both of which had been purchased by her mother and both of which were at least a size too small. "Come on," her mother beckoned, turning around to her daughter in annoyance. "Chop-chop."

As April caught up, her mother pushed her ahead of her at the door. April flinched as her mother began to pat down her hair. "Flyaway hair," she muttered, as her dad rang the doorbell. April plastered a smile on her face as Mrs Walsh appeared in the doorway. Her parents did the same. Happy families posing for a portrait, April thought.

Mrs Walsh shook hands with them all and hugged April to her large bosom before ushering them all into the kitchen. "Sit down, sit down," she said, indicating the kitchen chairs, as she went to put on the kettle.

There was nowhere to sit, all the chairs were covered in clothes or newspapers.

Mrs Gavin gingerly removed a huge pile of ironed underwear from her chair and looked for somewhere to put it. She eventually placed it on the ironing-board which was standing in the centre of the kitchen. She perched herself delicately on the seat's edge.

Mrs Walsh grinned as she gestured around the room. "Sorry about the mess, I'd no choice but to iron today. Sarah was moaning that she'd nothing to wear, then she tried to iron her best shirt and burnt a hole right through it." She laughed as she pointed at herself. "And I got the blame," she announced, "me." She put a plate of biscuits in the centre of the table. "Kids, huh?" she finished.

"Indeed," Mr Gavin replied lamely.

"I usually get a lady in to clean and iron," Mrs Gavin mused, "I never liked housework." She paused, considered and finished, "I'm just not the stay-at-home sort, I suppose."

Mrs Walsh poured them each a cup of tea. "Can't stand housework myself," she said cheerfully. "Just 'cause I'm at home doesn't mean it gets done." She laughed and, without waiting for a response, she turned to April. "How'd you like the idea of living in Dublin? It'll be a change for you."

April shrugged. "Don't mind." She gave Mrs Walsh a quick smile and looked down at the table again.

"I hope you won't be too homesick," Mrs Walsh continued. She felt as if she was trying to squeeze blood from a stone: the child was as shy as a three-year-old.

"I'll be fine," April muttered, her face flushing crimson.

"April's very adaptable," Mrs Gavin said brightly, patting her daughter on the head. "She'll be fine." She smiled at Mrs Walsh. "She's well used to strange places."

"So I believe." Mrs Walsh didn't sound impressed.

"Jim and I are away quite a lot. It's not good to have your children with you all the time – they need their

13

own space. Teenagers, especially. April benefits from the experience."

"Really?" Mrs Walsh sounded sceptical.

Jim Gavin thumbed to his daughter. "Oh, yes," he said heartily, "I've introduced April to so many interesting people. It broadens the mind, you know." He looked at his daughter. "Isn't that right?"

"Yeah." April was concentrating on her tea. She began to crumble a biscuit between her fingers.

"April," her mother snapped, "will you stop that, there's crumbs everywhere."

April stopped and shoved the biscuit in her mouth.

"Don't worry about crumbs," Mrs Walsh smiled. "This place is in a permanent state of chaos."

The Gavins looked at her blankly and so she went on hastily, "Sorry that the rest of the crew aren't here. Sarah went into town with her boyfriend, and Jack is at . . ." She stopped abruptly as the front door was slammed violently shut, making the Gavins jump.

"Only us," a male voice yelled and Mr Walsh strode into the kitchen, followed by a mucky-looking individual in a track suit who was concentrating on holding a filthy rag up to his nose. There was blood pouring on to the rag and the person exclaimed, "Me nose thinks it's a bleedin' tap."

Father and son began to chortle at the pun.

Mr and Mrs Gavin looked faintly disgusted. April tried her best not to smile.

Mrs Walsh was mortified. What an introduction!

"Jack," she exclaimed. "What happened?"

"We won is what happened," Jack grinned around at them all then. "How's it goin'?"

"Hello," Mrs Gavin said faintly.

14

April gave a shy smile and her dad nodded.

"Good game?" Mrs Walsh asked her son.

Jack sat astride a chair. "The best," he confirmed. "Two-nil, into the quarter-finals of the cup now." He began to mop his nose and then he reached out a dirty hand and took three biscuits from the plate.

Mrs Gavin made a mental note not to eat any more biscuits.

Jack nodded amicably at them all. "Sorry I can't shake hands," he apologised. "I'm manky. The showers broke down."

"Go and get cleaned up," Mrs Walsh ordered and as he left the kitchen, she turned to the Gavins saying apologetically, "He's not usually as bad as that."

"Yeah, he's usually worse," Mr Walsh half-joked, half-grumbled. He then began to tell them all about the football match.

April couldn't believe that this man was in any way related to her dad. They were so totally different. This was the "Dan the Man" her Dad visited every so often in Dublin.

Dan Walsh was animated in his discussion of his son's team. Ballinteer United were on the up, according to him. April learned that Jack had played a blinder and scored from a corner – whatever that was. Luke – whoever he was – was a great midfielder – whatever that was – and had scored one as well. "The next cup match is not for another three weeks," Mr Walsh announced as he studied the calendar. April wondered what on earth a cup match was.

At 5.00 Mr and Mrs Gavin left. April knew they would leave early. She could see her mother growing bored by all this sport conversation and her dad liked to be at least two hours early for every journey he took.

They were left alone in the kitchen to say their goodbyes. "Now," her mother said as she fussily straightened April's hair yet again, "eat well, won't you?"

April nodded.

"Try not to pick up that horrible Dub accent," Mrs Gavin smiled.

April managed to smile back at the feeble joke.

"Take care, won't you?"

Again April nodded.

There was an uncomfortable silence. Mrs Gavin turned away after briefly touching her daughter's cheek. "I'll be in the car," she said to her husband.

Mr Gavin watched his wife leave. Then he turned to his daughter. "Now, remember, study hard." He stopped and nodded. "It pays off in the end." He looked at her and bit his lip, rocking to and fro on his heels. "Still," he smiled. "I don't have to tell you that, do I?"

"No."

"I wish you were coming with us." He paused, waiting for her to say something and, when she didn't, he took an envelope from his jacket pocket.

"I've gone through all your school-books and made out a study time-table for you to follow. It's easy to keep on top of things, you know." He was about to say more, then changed his mind. "Keep up the good work, huh?"

April merely nodded.

"Another doctor," he grinned proudly. "Gavin and daughter – sounds good, huh?" He stood there, smiling. Then he shook her hand and patted her on the back.

"See you, Dad," April whispered.

Remembering made April's eyes water. Her heart hurt and she wondered if she was sad or just relieved. She would miss them, but she was used to that. Something else was happening to her. She suddenly realised that she was a stranger in this place. No one knew her. No one knew what she was like. No one knew what to expect from her. It was a strange and alien but also a liberating feeling. She didn't have to be brainy April Gavin, or April Gavin, daughter of brilliant Doctor Gavin, or worse, "pass the parcel" April G any more. She was in Dublin now, no one knew her here – maybe here she could just be April Gavin, just herself.

Chapter Five

The sun, sneaking through a chink in the bedroom curtains, woke Sarah the next morning. It was bright for a January day and thin rays of sunlight slanted across the room. They lit up Noel Gallagher's face and Sarah blew him a lazy, grinning kiss. She stretched and savoured the silence of early morning. She never got up on a Sunday till at least noon, so she could either fall asleep again or just luxuriate in the sleepy drowsiness of waking. Turning over to check what the time was, she was jolted fully awake by the sight of the girl sleeping in the spare bed. She had forgotten that April "swot" Gavin, as they had nicknamed her, was sharing her room for the next nine months. Sarah gazed over at April. She didn't quite know what to make of her. It was puzzling. Sarah was fond of making snap judgements on people and prided herself on being a good judge of character. April had been a mystery. She wasn't real brainy-looking, she wasn't the classic swot. In fact, Sarah had been pleasantly surprised upon meeting April. She was even quite good-looking – not the thick glasses and fuzzy hair type at all. She wasn't skinny but she wasn't fat, either. Her hair was brown, as were her eyes. She was a bit shy, though.

Jack had said that April reminded him of a rabbit caught in the glare of car headlights, scared-looking –

which was about as profound as Jack would ever get. Sarah felt a bit envious of her brother's comment. Trust Jack to say what she herself had been thinking. He only did it to annoy her.

She pushed Jack from her mind, even the thought of him set her on edge. Instead she refocused her attention on April. It was kind of exciting having a sister of sorts for nine months. Her only hope was that April would be a bit of a laugh. April stirred and, opening her eyes, gave Sarah her "rabbit" smile, as Jack called it. She would look at you for a second or two and then drop her gaze, as if embarrassed.

"What's the time?" she asked quietly.

"Almost ten."

April jumped as if stung. She reddened. "Oh, God, have I missed breakfast? Have I slept it out?" Her tone was apologetic.

"Relax," Sarah indicated herself. "Do I look as if I've been up for hours?"

April went even redder.

"Janey, no one in this house gets up before mid-day." She grinned broadly at April. "If you want, you can make the brekky, only you'll have to bring it to us all in bed."

April pulled the covers back over her legs. She glanced quickly in Sarah's direction as she said, "I was stupid. Sorry."

"Sorry for what?" Sarah was incredulous. "Sure, how were you to know? Don't be thick, just relax, lie back an' enjoy the next two hours."

"It's just that at home I'm usually up at nine on Sundays."

"Look, this is Dublin," Sarah answered, trying to make the girl smile. "In Dublin, do as we do. In Cork, they're all mad anyhow – that's the word on the street up here. The Cork culchies are crackers, you know? Gettin' up at nine on Sunday's insane!"

April's face crinkled slowly into a smile as she heard the word "culchie", a word Dublin people used to describe people from the country. "So, I've to blend in with the jackeens, is that it?" she quipped, using the Cork slang for Dubliners. She reddened again as she spoke.

Sarah managed a laugh. "Yeah, got it in one." She noted the way April's face registered relief that her joke had been laughed at. Sarah vowed that, no matter how bad April's jokes were, she was going to scream with laughter at them. She sat up in bed and, hugging her knees to her, asked sympathetically, "Did you manage to get any sleep at all last night?"

"Huh?"

"I can never sleep when I go somewhere new," Sarah confided. "I can only sleep in me own bed. Are you like that?"

April nodded. "Suppose." She floundered and eventually said, "I'll just have to get used to this bed, though, won't I?"

"Yep," Sarah grinned. Then, shrugging, she said, "Dublin's not so bad, you know, you'll like it. Ballinteer is great. If you get kinda weepy for the country, you can go to Marlay Park and walk in the fields and stuff."

"I hate fields," April smiled. "I hate hay and straw and the smell of . . . well, the horrible country smells."

"Cow shit?"

"Yeah," April nodded.

Sarah saw with some satisfaction that April was beginning to relax. She wasn't lighting up like a traffic signal every time she spoke.

"Look," Sarah said, in an effort to make her feel more relaxed, "I know you'll probably be homesick an' stuff, but like, it'll be fine."

April nodded and said softly, "Mum and Dad travel a bit, just short trips and stuff, but I'm used to them not being around."

Sarah nodded. "What about Cork, will you miss Cork?"

"God, no."

The fervour with which she said this startled both girls. April gazed at the wall with intense concentration. Sarah gawked at her.

"No?" she asked. "Why? Did you hate the place?"

Sarah waited for April to answer. It seemed to take an eternity. She was about to tell her that she was sorry to have pried when April turned toward her. She was grinning but it seemed to be forced. She said offhandedly, "Miss Cork? No – no talent. All horrors. I hear there's more men up here."

Sarah smiled, relieved that she hadn't upset April and yet feeling as if the humour wasn't quite real. She decided to play along, "Except for Frank, my fella, the lads here are awful as well."

April groaned. "And my dad told me that the guys were beauts. It was the only reason I agreed to come."

The idea of the sedate, earnest Dr Gavin advising his daughter on the merits of fellas was hilarious. Sarah and April grinned at each other.

"Jack and I are goin' out tonight, just to the local for a bit of crack – do you fancy comin' along?"

"Go out with you?" April said it almost reverently.

"Yeah," Sarah nodded. "Well, I'll be goin' on Frank's bike, but you can follow on down with Jack."

"Are you sure you won't mind me tagging along?"

"Tagging along?" she scoffed as she made a face. "Sure, you'll be one of the family for the next few months. Come on, it'll be a laugh."

April really grinned now. "Yeah," she said. "I'd like that."

All gawky. All woeful.

April had forgotten that her wardrobe was a fashion connoisseur's nightmare. God, what was she to wear out that night? Everything she had made her look overweight or nerdish. She decided at last on jeans and a big sloppy jumper. The jumper was the only thing that she had ever bought by herself. Her mother had hated it, of course, and told her it gave her no shape. That made April like it even more.

She slapped on a bit of make-up, brushed her hair and sat on the bed waiting for Sarah to arrive in. She hadn't the nerve to waltz down to the kitchen as if she had lived in the house for ages, even though Mrs Walsh had told her to treat the place like home.

"You right?" Sarah poked her head in the bedroom door. She nodded approvingly at April's jumper and asked her where she had bought it.

April reddened. The name of the shop flew out of her head. She shrugged, "Cork city, some shop, I can't remember."

"You've loads of stuff," Sarah was looking at the open wardrobe door. "God, you're so lucky. I've about . . ." she paused and considered, " . . . three decent things to wear."

"I've this," April pointed to the jumper. "I hate all the stuff in there."

"Why'd you buy it, so?" Sarah was gazing at the clothes in awe.

22

"I didn't," April mumbled, as if reluctant to go on, "My mum did."

Sarah gawked at her. "Your ma buys you stuff?" she breathed.

"Yeah," April said glumly, "only I hate it."

"Tell her that, so," Sarah said as she pulled a horrible skirt out of the wardrobe. She made a comical face as she exclaimed, "God, you'd have to be over thirty to wear this."

April gave a hopeless shrug.

"Still, this is nice." Sarah held up a suede waistcoat.

"If you're a size ten," April said gloomily. She looked at Sarah and said shyly, "It'd fit you – have it if you like. I never wear it."

"Serious?" Sarah asked and without waiting for a reply she tried it on over her denim shirt. She turned about in front of the mirror, viewing herself from all angles. "Thanks. It's gorgeous!" April smiled at her exuberance.

Sarah sat down, cross-legged on her bed. "Can I really have it?"

"Sure."

"Great." Sarah beamed at her. "What kind of stuff are you inta, then?"

April shrugged. Her eyes darted to and fro as she thought about the question. Eventually she said diffidently, "Loose stuff, baggy trousers, floppy shirts, mad hats, stuff like that."

"And you've nothing like that?"

"No."

"You should put your foot down and just buy what you like," Sarah advised.

April said nothing.

"Here," Sarah reached under her bed. She pulled out

a mess of papers, books and pens and, eventually, a squashed flat hat. Banging it back into shape, she asked, "Mad hats like this?"

April grinned. "Yeah – like that," she agreed and her smile grew broader as Sarah, shoving it at her, said, "Here, you wear it – I'll swap it for all the gear in your wardrobe."

"Done," April laughed delightedly as she placed the hat on her head.

There was a tapping on the door, and Jack strode into the room. "The Plank has arrived," he announced loudly. "He's sittin' in the kitchen waitin' for his chick."

"You shut up," Sarah whispered furiously. "Don't keep callin' him that." She pushed roughly past her brother and then, pausing at the top of the stairs, she continued, "And don't dare come into my room until I say so – right?"

Jack made a face at her retreating back and, turning to April, said, "Come on down and see this guy." He grinned hugely at her, his eyes dancing, "He's like something you only ever see once – an opportunity not to be missed."

April didn't know whether this was a joke or not. She gave Jack a quick smile and said, "Sarah says he's lovely."

Jack began to snigger. "You've gotta see this fella," he whispered, "'Lovely' is not the word. Sarah thinks he's so cool or somethin'." He grinned at her. "Come on quick, before they leave. She'll probably go on his bike to the pub."

April, curious now to meet the wonderful Frank, followed Jack downstairs and into the kitchen.

Jack pushed April in front of him as they entered and

24

she saw Frank kissing Sarah. She was mortified and was about to make a quick exit when Sarah spotted her. "April," she beamed, without a trace of embarrassment, removing her arms from around Frank's neck, "This is Frank." She cuddled up to Frank. "Frank," she cooed, "meet April."

"Hiya," April said timidly as she held out her hand, trying not to gawk. The only resemblance that this guy had to Brad Pitt was Brad's second name. He was the pits. Frank's long skinny body reminded April of a window pole. A window pole that was covered, head to foot, in tight leather. A window pole with long, matted hair and a small narrow face.

Frank looked April up and down. He held his hand in a peace sign and drawled, "Hey, how's it goin'?"

April didn't know what to do. She blushed furiously and let her hand fall to her side. "Grand," she faltered, "grand, I'm grand."

Frank then acknowledged Jack by saying, "How's ma man?"

"He's bisexual," Jack said in a undertone to April. "Sarah's his chick an' I'm his man."

A smile danced across April's face.

Aloud Jack drawled back, "Hey, Frank, I'm cool, man."

April was afraid she would laugh.

Sarah shot Jack a murderous look, but Frank didn't seem to notice. "Cool, Jacko. Nice ta hear."

The doorbell rang and Jack went to answer it. Loud greetings were exchanged and he arrived into the kitchen with another guy.

"This is Kev," Jack introduced him to April. Kev at least looked normal, if you didn't count his really, really red hair.

Kev held out his hand and shook April's vigorously. "How's it goin'?" he said in a flat Dublin accent. "Nice to meet you."

"You comin', babe?" Frank asked Sarah. "The bike's parked outside." He picked a helmet up off the floor and threw it at her. "Put that on your head, hon."

He sashayed his way to the door. He squeaked as he walked.

"Lookin' good there, buddy," Jack drawled again and Frank gave a gratified grin.

Kev and Jack began to snigger.

Sarah chose to ignore her brother. "Do you mind walkin' down with the two of them?" she asked April, nodding at Jack and Kev. "I'll wait if you want."

April shook her head. "No, you go on," she urged, desperately wishing that Sarah would stay, "I don't mind."

"Yeah, she'll be safe with me," Jack said. "I'll keep Kev away from her."

"Feck off, Walsh," Kev retorted. Then, laughing, he said to April, "His nickname in the clubs is 'Octopus'."

"Naw, that's Luke's," Jack protested and the two laughed. At April's puzzled look, he said, "Sorry, unfair joke; forget it, April."

"Talkin' of Luke, I told him to call in here. I said we'd walk down with him," Kev said.

Jack made a face. "Great, nice one, Kev. Is he in talkin' form tonight?"

Kev shrugged. "I hadn't a choice. He asked if we were goin' to the pub tonight and I said 'yeah'. He said he'd call in."

"Great," Jack said glumly. "He always puts everyone on edge."

April wondered vaguely who Luke was.

They waited ten minutes for Luke to show and, when he didn't, the three left, Kev and Jack grumbling about how unreliable Luke was.

April fumbled in the pocket of the jeans to make sure she had her money with her. Her dad had given it to her for emergencies and April figured that having no money to go out was a minor emergency in itself.

When they reached the pub, it was packed. They took a while to find their crowd and, when they did, there was just enough room to sit down. April was introduced to a dizzying array of people. There were guys on the football team and people from school. She just smiled around at them all and wished that she knew just one person really well. She searched desperately for Sarah but she was over the other side of the table gazing reverently at Frank. April sat down beside Jack and began to study the drink he'd bought her with a desperate interest.

"Are you the girl staying with the Walshes?" a girl on her left asked.

April nodded.

"I suppose it's hard for you, getting to know everyone?" the girl said sympathetically.

April gulped and took a deep breath. "Yeah," she stammered. "It's hard. I'm not the best at talking to strange people."

The girl grinned at her. "You couldn't get much stranger than the Walshes," she laughed. Then, holding out her hand she said, "My name's Jane, by the way. I knew you probably wouldn't remember it the way Jack gave you the whirlwind intro."

April found herself smiling back. This really wasn't so bad.

"AW, HERE HE IS!" Jack yelled, making April jump.

A tall dark youth pulled up a seat between April and Jack.

"Where the feck were you?" Jack asked. "We waited for ages – didn't we, Kev?"

"Yep," Kev nodded.

"Couldn't get away," the lad said. "I did call in to you but your ould fella said yez were gone."

Jack nodded and then, pointing to April, he said, "Luke, this is April from Cork – she's stayin' at our place for a while."

April, feeling slightly more confident, smiled. "Hiya."

Luke took a gulp of his pint, nodded curtly at April and turned around to talk to Jack again.

April, to her surprise, felt annoyed. There was no need for him to be so rude.

"He's our star player," Jack continued. "He set up a beaut for me yesterday."

April made the appropriate noises of admiration and then, because she felt she was expected to say something, asked, "Are you in school with the others? You kind of look older."

There was an awkward silence. Jack broke it by saying, "Naw, Luke left the year before last. He would've been . . ."

Luke cut him short. "Don't beat about the bleedin' bush, Walsh." He turned to April. "I didn't 'leave', I was, eh, forcibly ejected, shall we say." He studied her reaction.

April could feel a blush starting. But anger made her determined not to drop her gaze from his. "You mean you were expelled," she stammered.

Luke nodded. "Yep, right first time." His eyes mocked her; they reminded April of black holes, swallowing things up, giving nothing back.

"Why?" April asked. She felt under pressure to prolong the conversation. God, she wished Jack would interrupt.

Luke flinched. His eyes shifted. It was like dropping a pebble into water and seeing the ripples. The blank look returned. "Why was I expelled?" he repeated.

Jack and Kev began to talk then, trying to ease over the situation. Luke ignored them. He gazed up at the ceiling as if trying to recall something he had memorised. "I was, eh, uncooperative, unresponsive, foul-mouthed; you name it, I was it."

April nodded. "Pretty good reasons," she said. It was a stupid thing to say, but it was the only thing she could think of. She could hear Jack's sharp intake of breath, but she couldn't believe it when Luke gave an incredulous smile. Almost as soon as it appeared, it was gone.

Encouraged, April asked, "What did your parents think?"

Luke shrugged. "They were pretty mad," he said simply.

Jack couldn't believe this conversation. Luke was a bit unpredictable, he couldn't let it go any further. "You got a job, anyhow," he interjected.

Luke nodded. "Yeah, great feckin' job," he spat. He turned once again to April and explained, "I deliver sausages for Murphy's Meats. Well, I don't actually drive the van, but I go around with the driver, you know."

"You're a sausage salesman," April pronounced. There was a guffaw of laughter from Kev. He tried then to make it sound as if he was coughing. Jack tried to kick April under the table. He wished he had warned her . . .

Luke's eyes narrowed. He glared into his pint.

"I wasn't being funny," April protested. God, this was awful, she thought, in with both feet. She floundered. "If someone asks what you do, tell them you're a sausage salesman."

Jack was trying to think of a new subject they could talk about, but his mind was blank. He was amazed when a slow grin spread across Luke's face.

"Yeah," Luke agreed. "Sounds all righ'. Impressive even." He gave April his full attention, ignoring Kev and Jack. "So, you come from Cork," he stated.

April was feeling reckless. He liked her, this guy liked her! He was smiling at her. He thought she was funny. She felt drunk on the knowledge, intoxicated with the confidence it gave her. She opened her eyes, wide and innocent. "And they expelled you," she exclaimed. "God, it wasn't for stupidity, anyhow, you've got good retentive powers."

Luke gave a roar of laughter and immediately there was silence at the table.

Luke glared at them all and, thumbing in April's direction, he shrugged, saying, "Can I help it if the girl is funny?"

"She must be a pantomime," one fella said. "Makin' you laugh is about as impossible as Rovers winnin' the league."

"Thanks," Luke snapped.

Another uncomfortable silence at the table.

"Or Man United winnin' the Champion's League," Sarah piped up.

"Get lost," Jack sneered at his sister. "United are brilliant."

The atmosphere was restored and a slagging match began as to whether United were any good.

Luke grinned again at April. "I sure hope you're inta

30

football; you'd want to be, hangin' around with this crew." Then, focusing his gaze on her, he asked, "You're from Cork an' your name is April. What else is there to know?"

Now that she had his full attention, April was mortified. She was bound to say something dense. "Nothin' much," she muttered. Then, knowing that some other response was expected, she asked, "You got any other family?"

"Got a brother, much younger than me, he's five."

"That's a big difference."

Luke half-grinned. "Big mistake, more like. Mind you, I think me ma thinks that I was the mistake at the moment." He shrugged ruefully then, looking at his empty glass, he stood up. "Can I get you anythin'? I'm off to the bar."

"Another orange," April dug her hands into her pocket for change, but Luke waved her away.

"I'll buy, you're grand."

April nodded her thanks and watched his retreating back. She couldn't decide if she liked him or not, but she had her mind made up on one thing: he was definitely the most interesting fella there.

Sarah watched Luke leave for the bar and breathed a sigh of relief. Frank was regaling her with tales of his motor-bike exploits and she was getting just the tiniest bit bored; not that Frank was boring, she chided herself, it was just that she was not really into motor-bikes. She was just about to move over to April when she saw Jack sliding into Luke's seat beside April. Obviously Jack, like Sarah, had decided that enough was enough . . .

"How are you enjoyin' yourself?" Jack asked, as he pulled his drink nearer to him.

31

"Fine," April looked at him in surprise. He was almost squashing her, he was so close.

Jack flushed, moved slightly and asked, "Kev is goin' to the bar, do you want anythin'?"

April shook her head. "Luke is gone to get me an orange juice."

At that moment the orange appeared over her shoulder as Luke put it down in front of her. "For the lady," he grinned. He looked expectantly at Jack to move, but Jack sat there, refusing to budge. April muttered her thanks but Luke ignored her. He gazed at Jack, bit his lip and said, "Can I get in there?"

Jack indicated the seat he had vacated saying, "Sure, Luke, sit down. God, you're splashin' out tonight, aren't you – free drinks for April."

Luke gave him a sharp look, sat down in the empty seat and said, "Yeah, well, a bleedin' orange won't break the bank. Here," he shoved a packet of Dry Roast at April, "I gotcha these as well, like you asked," he finished hastily.

April took the peanuts and smiled at Luke as she replied, "It was salted I wanted, but they'll do, I suppose."

She was delighted to see him laugh and she began to laugh with him.

Jack studied both of them; the way Luke was looking at April made his heart pound. Trust Luke Coleman to start sniffing around. God, if April got involved with him there was sure to be trouble.

Chapter Six

"Oy! Coleman, get a move on."

Luke jumped. He had been in a world of his own and the voice of his driver, Jimmy, made him start.

"Yeah, yeah, sorry, Jim," he mumbled as he began to load the sausages and rashers into the freezer van.

It was Jimmy's turn to looked surprised. Never could he ever remember this sulky youngster apologising for anything. "Aw, forget it." Jimmy patted Luke on the back and observed how Luke froze. "Didn't mean ta shout at you," he continued warily. "We're just on a tight run today, you know?"

"Yeah," Luke didn't look at him, he just kept on packing.

Jimmy began to help him. "How was your weekend?" It was a question Jimmy had been asking Luke every Monday for the past two years. He thought teenagers liked to talk about what they did at weekends. Luke always gave the same almost inaudible "All righ'" and the conversation would end.

Jimmy felt that he had done his duty and would then regale Luke with his own exploits, which usually revolved around telling the wife he was going out for a pint and rolling home at three in the morning. For some reason, Luke never really laughed at his stories; he might grin, but he never laughed. Jimmy wondered if Luke liked him at all.

"Well, the weekend?" Jimmy repeated himself, the kid wasn't with it today. "How'd it go?"

"Grand," Luke nodded at him. "The football team is into the quarter-finals of the cup."

"Oh yeah?" Jimmy tried to sound impressed. God, the kid was breaking out today. "What team do you support?"

"Naw, the team I play for," Luke explained as he shoved the last box into the van and slammed the doors shut. The two men went around and climbed into the van and Jimmy started it up. They were on a Galway run.

"Wha'? You play football. Who for?"

"Big team," Luke grinned. "Ballinteer United."

"Oh, them," Jimmy laughed. "Know them all right!" Coleman was in fine form today. Jimmy decided to find out all there was to know before the fella clammed up again. "Any good?" he asked.

"We're all righ'."

"Naw, you," Jimmy asked. "Are you any good? Wha' position do you play?"

Luke shrugged. "I'm all righ'. I'm supposed to be a midfielder, but I score a bit as well."

Jimmy nodded in approval. "Fair play, fair play. I never knew you played before." He didn't know what else he could say.

"Sure when I broke me arm, I couldn't play for ages." Luke rubbed his arm as he spoke.

"Any other news?" Jimmy had his eyes fixed on the road. He nodded his head toward the dash and Luke lit up a cigarette for him and shoved it between his teeth.

"Naw."

"Bleedin' great piece of road, this," Jimmy muttered as they headed on to the motorway. He put his foot down and the accelerator climbed to seventy.

Luke watched the road flash by and wished that they would let him drive the van just once in a while. Jimmy shoved in a T-Rex tape and began to warble along with it, in between telling Luke about the way his wife had locked him out Friday night. "I had to sleep under the flippin' car," he said savagely. "The oul bitch wouldn't let me have the keys to sleep in it. She was afraid I'd drive away an' me locked outa me tree."

Luke grinned at the right places, inwardly applauding Jimmy's wife. "She should've locked you out for a few more days," he felt like saying. Jimmy carried on a tirade against his wife as Luke let his mind wander back over what a good night he'd had last night. From the moment he had got up that morning to now, he hadn't been able to get April off his mind. He didn't know why he felt like this – it wasn't that she was gorgeous or anything, though she was all right looking. She had a nice accent and a good sense of humour, but there was something else . . . Luke tried to put his finger on it. It was when she had looked him in the eyes and asked why he had been expelled. Luke grinned at the memory. Jack and Kev had been planking. April wasn't afraid. That was it. She just wasn't afraid.

Luke liked her a lot.

Jimmy pulled the truck into Mother Hubbards and declared that they might as well get a sambo and a cuppa. Luke wondered what had happened to the "tight run" they were on but, feeling hungry himself, said nothing. Over tea, Jimmy began on his second favourite topic of conversation for the morning, the exploits of his sixteen-year-old son. He had got drunk on Saturday and Jimmy had given him a hiding.

Luke looked in disbelief at this man whose speciality act was drinking the bar dry each weekend. Did this guy ever listen to himself?

"I suppose the thump you gave him is ta make him stop?" Luke asked, eyes wide in mock innocence.

Jimmy wiped some mayonnaise off his lips and gave Luke a puzzled look. Was he being sarcastic or was the lad, as Jimmy so often thought, just plain thick? "'Course," he nodded vigorously. Pointing his finger at Luke he went on, "He won't dare come home like tha' again."

Luke let Jimmy munch his sandwich for a few seconds before dropping his bomb. "Didn't stop me."

"Huh?"

Luke shrugged, enjoying the look on his co-worker's face. "I came home drunk when I was thirteen. The oul' fella went ape. Didn't stop me."

Jimmy sneered. "I woulda stopped you, sunshine. Your ould man must be too soft altogether." He flexed his arm and glared at Luke. "I woulda stopped you," he repeated.

"I don't think so," Luke said softly. He smiled then at Jimmy and offered to buy them some crisps to take with them on the journey.

Jimmy accepted and Luke went over to the counter. "By God," Jimmy swore under his breath, as he looked at Luke paying for the crisps, "my son is not gonna end up a dead-beat like you, not if I have ta beat the sense inta him."

Chapter Seven

April glanced around nervously. Sarah had told her that she'd meet her outside the gym hall after school. It was nearly 4.30 now and Sarah still hadn't showed. April could feel people looking at her, she wondered if they were talking about her, if they thought she had been stood up. She took a deep breath, hoisted her bag on to her shoulder and began to walk toward the roadway.

She sighed with relief as she heard Sarah yelling her name. April turned around and smiled as Sarah jogged up to her.

Gasping for breath, Sarah said, "Sorry I'm late, the stupid teacher wouldn't let us out 'cause one of the lads was messin' in the class."

"Aw, don't worry about it," April indicated a nearby wall. "D'you want to rest for a sec?"

"Naw – let's get home, I think it's going to rain."

April pulled the hood of her jacket over her head as the first few drops began to splatter down.

"What did I tell you?" Sarah said mockingly as she twirled about, catching the rain on her palms.

"Singin' in the rain, singin' in the rain," a few lads sang as they passed by the two of them.

"If yez could sing it might be somethin', all right," Sarah yelled back.

The lads laughed loudly and began to jeer them but Sarah shook her head and turned laughing eyes upon April. "Ignore them now. It's best to pretend you don't hear them after you've made the smartest comment you can." She grinned. "It kills them."

April nodded. "I'll remember that," she smiled. She marvelled once again at Sarah's confidence.

"See you do," Sarah said, as the lads, growing tired of being ignored, sloped away. Sarah watched them leave. She winked, saying, "Treat 'em rough, they love it."

"Have you had loads of boyfriends, then?" April had the question out before she realised it. She blushed, saying hastily, "Sorry, I'm being awful nosey . . . "

"Will you stop saying sorry for everything," Sarah gave her a friendly shove. "I don't mind." She screwed up her face as she considered. "Only six, no, hang on, seven. Yeah, seven." She put her haversack on her back and shoved her hands into the pockets of her jacket to keep herself dry. "I've gone out with seven boys and only one man," she announced proudly. "Frank." She turned shining eyes on April. "Don't you think he's just lovely?"

April hadn't liked Frank much. "Yeah, lovely," she agreed lamely.

"You a fella in Cork?" Sarah asked.

April shook her head. "Naw, already told you – horrors." Sarah saw that funny look again on April's face. Any time Cork got mentioned, April's jaw would tighten. She decided to change the subject.

"How'd your first day go?"

"Grand," April nodded. "But the school, it's huge, I'll never find my way about."

"Aw, you will," Sarah assured her. "It's not as big as

it looks. When I was in first year I got lost all the time, now I can go about blindfolded."

"I hope you're right," April said. "My sense of direction is woeful."

"Someone told me you're doin' all honours subjects?"

"Yeah."

"God," Sarah sounded awestruck. "You must've done great in the Junior, what'd you get?"

"I did OK."

"Yeah, but like, what were your results like?" When she saw April's reluctance she urged even more, "Aw, go on, April, tell us."

"Five As, four Bs," April said in a voice barely above a whisper.

Sarah was gobsmacked. "Wow! That's good," she said reverently. "I only got one A and a few Bs and a C and a lot of Ds. Jack did even worse, but he doesn't care. Da said that if Jack were any more laid back he'd stop breathin'."

April began to laugh. She thought the Walshes were gas.

Sarah looked at her in surprise. April had a nice laugh. She grinned. "I wish he would stop breathing," she declared. "Make life a whole lot easier for me."

"Don't say that," April was still smiling. "He's not the worst."

"Did you swot a lot for it?" Sarah was back to exam conversation. She noticed again the way April tensed up. She decided to change the subject before the girl got any more uncomfortable. "You shoulda seen Jack givin' his results to me Da," she laughed. "He handed him the results and skedaddled. Da just looked at them and muttered 'Typical' or somethin'. That was the end of it."

April shook her head. "God, my dad wouldn't be like that."

"No?"

"No," April said in a tone that meant the conversation was closed.

Sarah informed her that Jack wanted to be a mechanic and that she wanted to go into modelling. "Da won't let me put me name down with an agency till I leave school," she moaned. Then, looking in admiration at April, she said, "You want to do medicine, don't you?"

There was a moment's silence before April stuttered, "Eh, yeah."

The rain was pelting down now and both girls began to run. They were soaked by the time they reached the house. Sarah unlocked the front door. "Cuppa?" she asked as she went into the kitchen. "I always have one when I come in."

"Join you in a sec," April said. She just wanted to get away from Sarah for a minute. Her heart was pumping, her throat dry. Slowly she made her way upstairs, her mind reeling.

Opening the door of the bedroom, she sat wearily down on the bed and tried to work out how she felt but couldn't. Nothing seemed to make any sense. The questions, the endless questions . . . She felt as trapped here as she had in Cork. She wanted to scream; it was hard when you screamed inside and no one heard. The pictures she drew made no sense to anyone except her. April took them out from her art folder and studied them. Cartoon pictures – a potter scratching his head in annoyance at a cup that did not want to be a cup, wanted instead to be part of something greater. High fences of evil stinging nettles separating good land from bad. Horses with sad eyes that were forced to drink muddy water. April loved and hated these pictures, they were how she felt. They were part of her.

She knew she could tear them up if she wanted to or she could force change on them. If only she could grasp the nettle that was her life. If only things were that simple . . .

"Sarah made a flippin' show of herself last night," Jack announced over dinner.

Mr Walsh began to cough violently and Mrs Walsh looked in horror at her daughter. Sarah told Jack to get lost.

" . . . She was all over that leather-bound motor-bike maniac," Jack grinned at his sister and winked at April.

"I WAS NOT," Sarah shrieked. "I never did anything to be ashamed of, so there." She felt like flinging her fork at him, but announced instead, "Just cause you've no one who wants to go out with you . . . "

"Correction," Jack said sweetly. "I don't wanna go out with anyone. If I did, I'd have no problem pickin' up a bird."

"Jack," his mother said sharply. "Don't use the word 'bird' when you're talking about girls."

Jack shrugged. "A mot, then," he amended.

"Thick," Sarah said scornfully. "Grow up, Jack."

"Any one that necks their fella in public better grow up themselves," Jack said casually as he scooped a large spoonful of ice cream and put it in his mouth. He grinned amicably at his mother and father's shocked faces. Then, holding up his hands, he said, "Joke?"

"It better be," Mr Walsh grumbled, looking daggers at his daughter.

"Unfortunately it is," Sarah giggled and April

laughed as well. "Frank isn't like that," Sarah continued and hastily added, "Neither am I, Ma."

"I hope not," Mrs Walsh looked troubled. She didn't like Frank very much. Frank the Plank, Jack was right about that at least.

"Did you have a good time?" Mr Walsh turned to April. "What do you think of the company they keep?" He nodded at his two children.

"Great time," April smiled. She noticed the four looking at her and stammered, "Everyone was very friendly."

"Especially Luke," Sarah teased. She turned to her father. "Do you know he actually bought her a drink, Da? He never buys a drink for anyone!"

"I'm impressed," Mr Walsh said. "It must be the start of a great love."

"Ha, ha," Sarah punched her da on the arm. She turned to April, saying, "He did take a shine to you, you know. I wouldn't go near him though, if I were you."

"It was only a drink," April protested, mortified.

"Terribly sulky young fella," Mr Walsh observed. "Seems angry half the time and the other half just plain scared to death. Drives me mad. I don't know why you hang round with him." The last part was directed at Jack.

Jack shrugged. "He hangs round with me," he corrected. "Anyhow, he can be all right sometimes. Still," he said, turning to April, "don't get too friendly with him – he's trouble."

"He only bought me a drink," April protested again. She wished they would stop looking at her.

"That's good for Luke," Sarah announced. "He's scabby."

"Just 'cause you don't like him . . . " Jack replied and

42

then said, "Sure you can't talk – the Plank isn't exactly Mr Generosity either."

"Dad, tell Jack to leave me alone!" Sarah appealed to her father.

Mr Walsh sighed. Turning to Jack he hissed, "Drop it, son."

"Yes, Pops," Jack replied as he grinned at April.

She was glad that the attention was off her.

The sound of a phone ringing stopped the chat. Mr Walsh went out to answer it and came back saying, "April, for you: your dad."

April went out to the hall and picked up the receiver. Her father's voice was crystal-clear, almost as if he were beside her.

"How's my girl?" he asked and April knew he was smiling. Despite herself she smiled as well. "Grand – I started school today."

"And?"

"It's fine. Jack and Sarah are fine."

"Didn't I tell you you'd like it?" Mr Gavin sounded triumphant.

"Yeah, you told me that all right."

There was a bitter edge to her voice that made her father say anxiously. "Are you sure things are fine?" Without waiting for an answer he continued, "I hope they take their work seriously in that school. Do they know they've a genius in their midst?"

"I think – "

He cut her short. "Listen, your mother's here, I'll put her on."

"Hello, darling," her mum's voice wafted like perfume down the line.

"Hi."

"They looking after you all right? You settling in all

right? I'm sending you some money for your birthday next week. Let me know if it arrives. I want you to buy something nice with it. I miss you, April. Can't wait to see you again. Just remember – eat sensibly. You are what you eat, you know!"

"I know." April made a face.

"Lots of hugs and kisses." Her mother blew a kiss down the phone and April heard her father yelling "Goodbye" somewhere in the background.

The line went dead.

Chapter Eight

"April!" Jack bellowed. "Shift yerself, willya!"

April pounded down the stairs, pulling on a cap as she did so. Her art folder, containing her sketch pad and pencils, was tucked under her arm. "Sorry," she gasped. "I couldn't find my pencils anywhere. Have I held you up?"

"Naw," Jack grinned, opening the door for her, "I'm usually late for trainin' anyhow."

The two began to walk briskly toward Marlay Park. Jack was going to football training and April was hoping to do some sketching.

Sarah had seen April's drawings in her art folder and had been raving about them. April had confessed to her that she wished she had somewhere she could sketch in peace. So, after careful consideration, Marlay Park had been decided upon. "There's a house there that's really nice," Sarah had said. "You might like to sketch it." Jack then promised to take her up to the park the following Saturday, when he went football training.

April was running in order to keep up with Jack's long strides. By the time they reached the front entrance, she was exhausted. "I'll have to get fit," she gasped, plonking down on a seat.

Jack laughed, slagging her over her red face. Then,

he said, "There's the house Sarah was on about." He pointed at the old house that dominated the park. "If you want you can wander around; you'll find it hard to get lost if you just keep going straight ahead. Eventually you'll end up back here, the park is in kind of a circle."

April nodded but knew that she'd just stay put. Jack had no idea just how bad her sense of direction was. She began to flip over the pages of her pad.

"See you in a couple of hours, so." Jack waved at her as he jogged off.

April watched him leave. Then, taking a deep lungful of fresh Marlay Park air, she began to draw.

Luke needed to get out.

The house was oppressive.

He glanced at his watch and decided that, if he left right at that minute, he could still make it for the last hour of football training. Shoving his kit into his sports bag, he took the stairs two at a time.

"Goin' out," he yelled to his ma. When she didn't reply, he poked his head around the kitchen door. "Goin' out," he repeated.

"See ya," his ma replied. Turning toward him, she asked, "Will you be back for tea?"

"Should be."

"Bye, Luke," Davy said.

Luke grinned at his younger brother. "I'll bring you back somethin'," he promised. "An apple or somethin'." He laughed as Davy's face filled with disappointment. "OK," he amended. "A bar of somethin'."

"A Snickers?" Davy asked hopefully.

"Yeah, right, so," Luke nodded. He laughed at Davy's "Oh Yes!" Once outside, he began to run. The park wasn't that far away and he made it to the front entrance

46

in under ten minutes. He was walking toward the pitches when a girl caught his eye. She was sitting opposite the old house, her head down, her brown hair falling over her face.

Luke shielded his eyes against the strong winter sun to get a better view. He was convinced it was April, the girl that was staying with Jack's folks. He really liked her, she was the kind of girl you could talk to. The only girl that talked to him, anyhow, he thought ruefully.

Luke decided to walk past to see if it was her.

It was.

"How's it goin'?" he said, smiling and sitting down beside her.

April jumped. "God, you frightened the life out of me," she laughed, her face going crimson.

"What you doin'?" Luke asked, now totally lost for something to say. He never normally went out of his way to chat up girls. He avoided them if at all possible.

April tried to cover her picture. "Aw, nothing; just, you know, well, just drawing." She tried to stuff her sketch into her folder.

"Oh, yeah?" Luke bit his lip. What next? "Eh, drawin' what?"

"The house, trees . . . " April indicated the view.

"Yeah?"

"Yeah."

"Mind if I have a look?"

Reluctantly, April handed her picture to him. "It's just a rough sketch," she muttered. "I'll do it up better when I get back."

Luke looked at the pencil drawing. "It's really good," he said, impressed. "You don't look the paintin' type."

April smiled. "Thanks." She put the picture back in her folder.

"You goin' to paint any more of the park?"

April nodded. "I might, only I don't know my way around it. I'm hoping Jack'll give me a guided tour one day."

"I'll give you the guided tour today, if you like," Luke was desperate to keep her talking.

"But don't you have practice or something?" April nodded toward his sports bag.

"I'm so late I've missed most of it, anyhow," Luke grinned. Then, shrugging, "Well?"

April gulped. The guy had a bad reputation. But he looked so nice, and those eyes. . . April liked his eyes. And she had finished her sketching for now. "Lead on, so," she said shyly, "Show me all the best places for pictures."

"At your service," Luke gave a mock bow and indicated the pathway. "After you."

"A guide with manners – I'm impressed," April joked.

Luke laughed. "The manners are a fiver extra, didn't I mention tha'?"

"Drop them, so."

They both grinned and began to walk. He showed her as much of the park as he could without wandering over too near the football pitches. "Bill'd feckin' kill me if he knew I was here," he said as he sauntered on ahead of her.

April grinned at his easy attitude. The guy didn't give a toss for anything. She liked that.

After about forty minutes, they arrived back where they had started.

"Tour over," Luke said.

April smiled. "Thanks. Thanks a lot." She tapped her

folder. "I'll be up here every Saturday from now on, scribbling away."

"I'll defo have to go trainin' from now on, so," Luke laughed. He could have bitten his tongue off when he saw the mortified look on April's face. He turned from her. "I, eh, I better be headin' off," he mumbled. "You goin' for a drink tonight?"

April nodded.

"See you there – all right?"

"Yeah, see you," April watched him leave. She felt like a right thick, imagine getting embarrassed just 'cause the guy made a joke. God, he probably thought she was an awful eejit and the worst part of it all is that he'd be right.

"You eejit, April," she whispered angrily as she flopped down on to a seat and began her wait for Jack.

Chapter Nine

April received fifty pounds from her parents for her birthday. They also sent her two theatre tickets.

Sarah grinned at her as she opened the registered letter. "Wow, fifty quid. What you gonna buy?"

April shrugged. "Dunno," she muttered as she pocketed the cash. "I'd like to get some decent clothes and stuff, but I don't really know Dublin."

"I'll go with you if you like," Sarah offered. We can go tomorrow, it's a half-day." She looked at April hopefully.

April smiled. "Well, yeah, that'd be great," she agreed. "But don't think you have to go, just 'cause of me."

"Sure, it'll be torture helpin' you spend your cash but someone's gotta do it." Sarah laughed, putting her arm around April's shoulder. "I love shoppin'," she continued, "I *want* to go, all right?"

"All right," April smiled gratefully at her. "Thanks."

"For what?" Sarah scoffed. "Don't be mad." She shook her head and said emphatically, "Your problem is you're too polite. Don't keep sayin' sorry an' don't keep thankin' everyone."

April didn't smile back. She looked Sarah in the eye and repeated seriously, "I mean it, though, Sarah. Thanks." Turning on her heel she left Sarah open-mouthed in the hall.

"AND YOU'RE TOO BLOODY SERIOUS AS WELL," Sarah yelled after her.

She heard April laugh and grinned to herself.

The next day was a half-day and at 1.00 the two girls boarded the 48A bus and arrived in town forty minutes later. Sarah dragged April from shop to shop, offering advice and smart comments. Eventually the two selected black leggings, a long black button-down skirt and a black body-top. The hat was the find of the day – a large wine-and-black cap. Both of them were delighted with it and April promised that Sarah could borrow it if she wanted.

Laughing, Sarah linked her arm with April's, saying, "Why couldn't I have had a sister instead of a brother?"

"Why couldn't I have had a brother or a sister?" April replied.

"Nah," Sarah tossed her head. "I think you're lucky to be on your own. Imagine, all the attention for yourself. No one to fight with. I'd love it."

"I think you'd find someone to fight with anyway," April joked.

Sarah looked at her in amazement. "Feck's sake," she said with mock severity, "just 'cause you've new gear, you think you're great."

April laughed and Sarah grinned back.

She thought that April had changed in the few weeks that she had been in Dublin. Nothing major, just small things. When someone talked to her, April didn't go as red as before, nor did she jump in her chair. She even made jokes every so often. Sarah felt proud of the part she had played in making April more relaxed. Of course, to be fair, it was probably not just her, it was her ma and da, even Jack. Even that thick, Luke Coleman. Sarah winced. Even him. Her temper boiled every time she saw Luke talk to April. And talk to her he did, any chance he got. Everywhere they went now, Luke arrived on the scene. He always sat as near as he could to April and chatted away to her. April made him laugh; she was the first person ever to do that as far as Sarah was concerned. No one could believe it and, despite all the warnings, April just said, "We only talk, he's funny you know." Sarah knew that if Luke showed his true colours, April would be back to her introverted self. She felt protective toward April and she knew that, if Luke did anything to shatter her fragile ego, she would have it out with him, just like she should have done two years ago.

" – Bewley's?"

Sarah was startled out of her reverie. "Sorry, what did you say?"

"I said, I'm taking you for a cuppa in Bewley's as a 'thank you'."

"There's no need. I told you, I love shoppin'."

April ignored her. She marched ahead and when they entered the café she pointed to an empty table and said, "Hang on here and I'll get the coffee."

April waited until Sarah had almost finished her coffee before asking hesitantly, "Do you fancy coming with me to the play, Saturday week?" She held up the two tickets her parents had sent her.

"Aw, sorry, April," Sarah said regretfully, "I've to go out with Frank that night. I think it's his sister's 21st birthday or somethin'. I'm sorry."

"Don't keep saying 'sorry'," April grinned. "You're too polite." Then, gazing at the tickets, she said, "It's all right. I'll go on my own."

"Ma would never let you go into town at night on your own," Sarah was horrified. "Ask Jack; he'll go, I'm sure."

"I don't think a play would be his scene," April tried to appear tactful.

Sarah laughed. "'Course it won't. Imagine him at a play – God, I'd love to see it! Go on, April, ask him, please."

April shook her head. "Oh, I couldn't do that," she gulped.

"Aw, go on," Sarah was an expert wheedler. "Please?"

"I don't think . . ."

"Please?"

April thought for a moment. She didn't want to, but then again, it was the story of her life.

"All right," she whispered. "All right."

"So you'll ask him?"

"Can't wait."

Sarah began to choke on her coffee.

They decided that it would be best if April were to ask Jack at the dinner table. That way he couldn't squirm out of it. "Ma will make him go," Sarah said, exulting in the possibility of Jack having to suffer a night at the theatre.

Jack had just told a school story that caused everyone except Mr Walsh to crease up laughing. "I don't think that story is exactly a great reflection on you," he muttered angrily.

"April wants to ask you somethin', Jack," Sarah kicked April under the table and then turned her face away so she wouldn't laugh.

"Yeah?" Jack turned his blue eyes on her.

April swallowed. Her face began to burn. This wasn't a bit funny. "Eh, I was wondering if you'd come out with me, Saturday week?" Then, seeing his questioning look she clarified, "Not on a date or anything like that. I got two tickets from my parents to go out that night and I need someone to go with."

"'Course he'll go," Mr Walsh beamed at April. "He'll

be delighted to go." Just what the lad needs, he thought, a nice quiet girl.

Jack nodded. "Yeah, sure, I'll go. Where are you goin'?"

"Theatre," April mumbled. She heard Sarah dissolving into quiet laughter beside her.

"Huh?" Jack put down his mug of tea. "As in a play, like?"

"He'd love it," Mrs Walsh stated firmly. She kicked Jack under the table.

"Sarah might like it better," Jack tried to say magnanimously.

"Can't go." Sarah tried not to splutter. "I'm goin' out with Frank that night."

"How convenient," Jack shot her a murderous look.

"Yeah, well, if you could find someone desperate enough to go out with you, maybe you wouldn't have to go to a play."

April could have died. "He doesn't have . . . "

Jack cut her short. He tried not to appear horrified, he knew that she had set him up. "I'd rather go to the theatre than feckin' go out on a date with an icon from the sixties," he said calmly. He ignored Sarah's intake of breath as he turned to April. "I'll go," he said as graciously as he could, "on condition that you come to our cup match that Saturday afternoon."

"He'll go with you anyhow," Mr Walsh said sharply. "If April is nice enough to ask you out, than you *will* go." He directed this at his son.

April grinned with relief. "No, it's all right, Mr Walsh," she said. "I'd love to see this wonderful football team in action. I'll go, Jack."

He grinned at her. "Sarah, get knittin' that scarf."

Sarah bristled but, upon seeing her Dad's warning look, she said nothing.

Chapter Ten

Jack dug out a manky blue-and-white scarf for her and Sarah lent her a hat. "Team colours," she grinned as she stuck it on April's head.

April felt a bit stupid but a deal was a deal. Mr Walsh was driving them to the game, which was to be held in Marlay Park.

"You'll love it," Sarah enthused, "This match is a cup game and that makes it even more excitin'."

"I can't wait," April joked.

Sarah carried on undaunted. "A cup game is a knockout game. That means whichever team loses today is out of the competition. This game is a quarter-final. If Ballinteer win, it's the semi-finals – the furthest they've ever got."

She then went on to explain about the league. "Each team in the league plays a 'home' and an 'away' match against every other team. If a team wins a match, they get three points; if they draw a match, they get one point. If they lose, they get no points. At the end of the season, the team with most points wins the league." She sighed, "Our lads haven't a hope this year. They had too many injuries. Luke was missin' for months when he broke his arm. Still," Sarah folded her arms against the cold as they left the warmth of the car, "he arrived back in the nick of time for the cup."

April's head was spinning: she really hadn't much of a clue what was going on, nor did she really care. She was surprised to see a fairly large crowd gathered when they reached the pitch.

"All the mammies and daddies," Sarah grinned.

The match started at 3.00, and it was freezing cold. Sarah pointed out all the lads on the team to her. "Jack, he's number 10, he's a striker, along with Luke, though Luke also plays midfield."

She waved over to Jack, who waved back. Luke waved over to them as well.

"God, you're well in there," Sarah commented dryly.

"Can I help it if I've a devastating effect on men?" April said nonchalantly. She was relieved when Sarah smiled. She couldn't understand why everyone seemed to dislike Luke. He was a good laugh, good storyteller, good company. April liked him more than she dared admit. Sarah wouldn't explain, either, just kept saying that he was dangerous. April wasn't prepared to shun him because of a few half-baked –

"See Kev, over there on the wing?" Sarah's voice broke into her thoughts. "He's a defender, he tries to stop the goals going in."

"I do have some idea what 'defender' means," April laughed. "I'm not totally thick."

Sarah shrugged. "Sorry," she grinned. "It's hard to tell sometimes."

April gave her a dig and she dodged, laughing.

The lads took up their positions on the pitch, the ref blew his whistle and the match began.

Sarah's voice could be heard all over the pitch as she

56

yelled and screamed out instructions to the players. She kept yelling for them to "Mind their houses".

Bill, the trainer, shrugged and grinned over at Mr Walsh. His team couldn't hear a word he was saying with the racket Sarah was making. Mr Walsh gave her a warning to shut up but she ignored him.

April stared at Sarah in amazement. What a voice! Feeling slightly embarrassed, she moved nearer to Mr Walsh. She didn't want people thinking it was her that was doing all the shouting.

Ballinteer got the ball early in the first half and missed a sitter. Sarah went berserk. "YOU STUPID THICKS," she yelled out to her brother. "ARE YEZ BLIND OR WHA'?"

Jack made a face at her and promptly missed another chance to the groans of all the spectators.

Sarah began to jeer. "Get him off, get him off, get him off," she sang.

April and Sarah ate themselves laughing when Jack gave them the two fingers.

The game began to settle down. April began to enjoy herself, biting her nails when it looked like Milltown Celtic might score. She even yelled a bit, though with Sarah beside her she was drowned out.

She had no problem spotting Luke. She couldn't help noticing him on the pitch. He seemed to be everywhere. "Luke is good, isn't he," she said to Sarah.

Sarah nodded. "Yeah, he's good, but a bit lazy today. He must've been out last night. Usually he'd have tried to score by this stage. He never turns up for trainin' or anythin'." She had her eyes fixed on the game, but was still intent on giving out about Luke. "I don't know how he stays so good – unreliable isn't the word."

April shook her head in disbelief. Imagine being so

talented and then not bothering to do anything about it – the guy was mad.

There were ten minutes to go and the match was scoreless. Sarah was anxiously pacing up and down the sidelines and cursing Ballinteer at the top of her voice. "YOU'LL NEVER GET THIS FAR AGAIN," she kept yelling. "COME ON, LADS!"

Suddenly, Luke got the ball and ran from the top of the pitch right down the middle with it. Even April could see the skill the guy had. He lobbed it into the penalty box where Jack took it down, he was just about to kick for goal when he was brought down by a terrible tackle.

"FOUL!" Sarah yelled along with the other supporters.

"PENO!" someone else called out.

The ref ran up the pitch, hand held out to award the penalty to the cheers of Ballinteer.

Jack still lay on the ground. There was a gang around him. "God, is he all right?" Sarah suddenly asked, growing pale. She ran onto the pitch, to the whoops and cheers of the crowd. She pushed her way into the middle of the group and the ref ordered her off the field of play.

"I'm not going till I find out if Jack is OK," she stated defiantly.

Jack, hearing his sister's voice, laughed and groaned at the same time. "Sarah, will you get off the pitch an' stop makin' a bleedin' show of me – I'm fine! I think I sprained me ankle."

"You mean that eejit from Milltown sprained it for you," Sarah yelled.

The "eejit" from Milltown took umbrage at this and told Sarah to "shut the feck up."

There was war.

Kev, coming to Sarah's defence, was pushed to the ground. He struck out and managed to catch the guy on the nose. Someone else rolled on top of the two of them and eventually the whole pitch was in uproar.

Kev's father, who had arrived to pick him up, shook his head.

"Trust Kev to be in the middle of it," was all he said.

Sarah, red-faced, marched off. "Animals," she fumed as her father asked her what had happened.

After about ten minutes, Jack hobbled off the pitch and Luke walked forward to take the penalty. The ball hit the back of the net to the ecstatic cheers of the crowd. Sarah jumped up and down and danced with a bewildered April up the sidelines. Mr Walsh and Kev's father laughed at the two of them.

"She'd make a holy show of you," Mr Walsh laughed as he ruffled his daughter's hair.

Kev arrived over when the final whistle went. He was covered in muck and blood. "Great match, huh?" he asked as he grinned at them. "I'm thinking of becoming a boxer – Steve Collins better watch out!"

Sarah looked sheepish. "Sorry 'bout that, Kev. The whole fight was my fault."

"Have to defend the lady's honour," he laughed. "Listen, I better go an' see how Jack is, I think his ankle is gone." He disappeared into the dressing-room to emerge a while later with a limping Jack in tow.

"He always gets injured," he thumbed at Jack. "If anyone is to get knocked about, it'll be him."

"You obviously haven't looked too hard at yourself in a mirror," Mr Boyle commented dryly. "You've a huge black eye on you."

Kev gingerly touched his face and flinched as his

hand touched the corner of his eye. "Ouch," he winced. "I knew it felt a bit sore, all right."

The others laughed as Kev departed with his father.

"Will you hang on for Luke, Da?" Jack asked as he put his kit in the back of the car. "I told him we'd give him a lift back."

"Sure," Mr Walsh helped his son into the front seat and they waited for Luke.

He arrived a few minutes later. "Sorry I'm late." He grinned at Mr Walsh and, turning to Jack, he said, "I had Bill chewin' me ear off. He thinks I played crap today." Changing the subject, he asked how April had enjoyed her first match.

"It was better than I thought it would be," April conceded. "Plenty of action, anyhow."

There was laughter and Sarah, giggling, said, "Let's hope Jacko thinks the same about his outing tonight." Turning to Luke, she said, "He's going to the theatre with April."

Luke looked at April, grinned and said wryly, "Well, I'm sure he'll enjoy it." Then he turned away and stared out the window.

Jack coughed and turned around. "Eh, April, please don't think I'm backin' away from my part of this bargain, but I honestly don't think I could go tonight. I can hardly even walk."

"Sure, sure," April grinned at him.

Sarah freaked. "Don't you dare back out," she snapped.

Jack held up his hands. "Honest," he pleaded. "I'd never do tha'." Then, pulling up his track suit at the ankle, he said, "Look, it's up like a bleedin' balloon."

"Then get a bleedin' wheelchair," Sarah said

sarcastically. "April has done her part of the deal, now you do yours." She turned to April. "Right?"

"Uh-huh," April mumbled uncertainly, feeling a bit sorry for Jack.

"Aw, come on . . ." Jack appealed.

"If you don't go, she'll have to go on her own," Sarah announced dramatically.

"You can't go into town on your own!" Mr Walsh exclaimed. "Absolutely not. It's too dangerous."

"Tell that to your son," Sarah was howling for blood.

"I'll go with you, if you're stuck." Luke had stopped gawking out the window and had taken an interest in the proceedings.

There was a silence.

"You?" Sarah unsuccessfully tried to hide the mocking tone in her voice.

"Yeah."

"You'd be more out of place than even Jack would be!"

"Thank you," Jack laughed. Then he turned to Luke. "You can rely on Sarah to be blunt."

Luke ignored them. "Well?" he shrugged as he gazed at April.

"Maybe Kev . . ." Jack tried to interject, but April cut him short.

This was one thing she wanted to do for herself and no one was going to tell her what to do. "You sure?" she asked Luke quietly.

"I'm free tonight, for a change," he grinned.

"Maybe Kev . . ."

April ignored the looks she knew she was getting from all the Walshes. She smiled at Luke. "Good, I'd like that. Come over about seven."

Chapter Eleven

Luke bounded downstairs. He was going to be late again. It was all his da's fault, as usual. Luke knew his da was in bad form because when Luke had got back from the match, his da had been in the front garden fiddling about with his car and cursing. He always did that on bad days.

Luke went into the television room where his ma and Davy were watching *Neighbours*. "I'm just goin' now, Ma," he said.

"She must be special."

Luke started. "Huh?"

"You've been smilin' a bit recently. I figured there had to be someone."

Luke shrugged. "There's no one," he grinned. Then, biting his lip, he asked, "Are you OK now?"

She nodded. "Don't worry about me. I'm fine. I've got Davy here to look after me." She smiled at her younger son. "You go and enjoy yourself."

"You sure?"

"Positive," she said and then, "Luke?"

He turned in the doorway and she said softly, "Treat her well, won't you?"

There was a silence and he nodded. "Yeah, 'course I will, Ma, 'course I will."

62

"Are you OK?" Sarah asked. April was acting in a peculiar manner. She was pacing up and down, up and down, and she kept looking at her watch all the time.

April said nothing, she kept on walking.

"April?"

"He's late," April tried to keep her voice steady. "He's late."

"It's only ten past seven," Sarah said calmly. "He'll be here." And if he's not I'll feckin' kill him, she privately thought.

"I said seven," April had stopped walking and was now sitting on the edge of her bed. "He said he'd be here at seven."

"Luke is always late," Sarah tried to make her voice sound calm and reasonable. "He's that sort of fella. Don't panic."

"I should have listened to you," April said, her eyes beginning to fill up. "You said he was unreliable."

Sarah couldn't believe this. April was going overboard. "It's only ten minutes," she repeated herself. "Give him a chance."

"It's a quarter past now," April's voice was rising. She took a deep breath and said, "He's not going to show. I just know it."

Sarah wished she could strangle Luke.

Luke began to run. He was already twenty minutes late and he knew that Sarah Walsh would be having a field day moaning on about how unreliable he was. He just hoped that April didn't believe her.

It was raining slightly and he shook his head as he arrived at the door in a feeble attempt not to look soaked. Trust him to forget his jacket. He looked down at himself, wondering if he was dressed right for a night at the theatre. He had put on his best black jeans and polished his Doc boots until they shone. His Ma had bought him a yellow grandfather shirt for his birthday and he had that on as well. He had his black, baggy jumper over his shirt. Luke took a deep breath and rang the bell.

Jack opened the door. "Late as usual, Coleman," he said, half joking, half in earnest. He was going to say more when Luke, knowing what was coming, said sharply, "April ready?"

Jack stared at him for a second before yelling, "April, he's here!"

April, with Sarah behind her, slowly made her way downstairs. He hadn't let her down. She didn't know whether to hug him or kill him.

"Hiya," Luke grinned. "Here I am."

April didn't smile in return. "I just hope we get there on time," she snapped as she stalked past him.

Sarah cheered inwardly. "Good on you," she thought. "Stand up for yourself, girl."

Jack gulped. He fully expected Luke to abandon her there and then but, to his surprise, Luke mouthed an "Ouch" and ran to catch up with April.

"Sorry I was late," Luke said as he fell into step beside her. "I couldn't help it."

April thought she was going to cry. She knew she was being stupid, but being stood up was something that terrified her. She tried to stop her voice from trembling by saying angrily, "If my night out is ruined, I'll blame you." She squeezed her hands together, felt her fingernails dig into her palms, and repeated, "I'll blame you."

"So, bleedin' blame me," Luke had raised his voice and upon receiving a curious look, lowered it. "I'm sorry I was late – what more can I say?" He put his hands in his pockets and turned from her.

There was silence between them until they boarded a bus.

"What's the name of the play we're goin' to?" Luke tried to start a conversation. He wasn't used to playing the role of peacemaker and it showed.

"*The Steward of Christendom*," April replied and, in an attempt to talk herself, said "It's got great reviews. I think we'll enjoy it."

"Who wrote it? Was it yer man – the Irish fella who wrote *The Van* and stuff? I like him."

April looked at him as if he had two heads. "No!" she said. "Roddy Doyle? You think Roddy Doyle wrote it?"

"Wrote what?" Luke was confused. "The play tonight or *The Van*?"

"Funny," April said and then, seeing that he actually hadn't tried to be funny, answered, "Sebastian Barry wrote the play we're going to."

"Never heard of him." Luke shrugged.

April sighed. To think she had been looking forward to seeing Luke tonight. Everything he had done so far was wrong. She glowered at him and said sarcastically, "Oh, well, if you haven't heard of him, why bother?"

Luke sighed. He had been looking forward to tonight but it looked like it just might be another disaster in what he called his life.

They arrived just as the play began. They were last on their row and everyone had to stand up to let them in. Luke insisted on saying "Thanks" to everyone they passed, which made even more noise. April kept her head down, afraid of the looks she knew they were getting from the "serious" theatre-goers. It seemed an eternity before they got into their seats. The play went well until Thomas Dunne, the main character, had his clothes removed on-stage. Another character proceeded to wash him down.

April was mortified. She couldn't bring herself to look at Luke. If she had been on her own she wouldn't have minded, but here she was with a guy she barely knew. April's hands began to sweat – it wasn't as if the play was crude or anything, but what on earth did Luke think of her going to see stuff like this?

"Now I know why you were mad to come here," Luke whispered in a laughing voice. "Jaysus, tryin' to corrupt me innocence."

April glanced at him and began to smile. "Maybe Sarah would've appreciated the view more," she giggled.

"After Frank, I'd say anything's an improvement." They both began to shake with laughter. Luke was told politely but firmly to "shut up" by an angry person behind him and that made them laugh even more.

Eventually April stopped giggling and turned to watch the rest of the play, a smile on her face.

Luke studied her profile. She looked lovely when she smiled, he thought. He spent the rest of the first half trying to figure out why he liked her. He kept looking at her out of the corner of his eye and wondering what it was about her that had him interested. He couldn't get her out of his head. He supposed it was the fact that she treated him as if he was just plain Luke Coleman – not Luke the expelled student or Luke the crook, as some people called him – she just treated him like anyone else.

Half-time came at last. Luke bolted from his seat, he was dying of thirst.

"Do you want somethin' in the bar?" he asked.

"An orange would be great," April said, following him. It took a few minutes to get the drinks. They found some seats and, just as April was sitting down, Luke handed her a packet of dry roasted peanuts and grinned.

April smiled back. "Salted," she slagged.

They grinned at each other. "Peace-offerin'," Luke said, nodding at the peanuts. He held out his hand. "Let's start over, huh?"

April shook his hand. "Yeah, I'm sorry for snapping your head off."

"An' I'm sorry for bein' late."

April shrugged. "I was just afraid you'd stood me up."

She wouldn't look at him.

"Stand you up?" Luke laughed. "God, I'd be mad to stand you up."

April stared at him.

He looked back. "I was mad when I heard Jack was bringin' you out."

April could feel a blush rising and covering her face. She hadn't a clue what to say.

Luke stared at her for a second or two more, then said, "Honest, I wouldn't let you down."

April shrugged. "Yeah, sorry. I, well, I got stood up before." She stopped and faltered as she tried to go on. "So that's why I was, you know, so uptight."

"Musta been blind or dumb or both."

"What?"

"The guy that stood you up – he musta been mad."

"I was pretty mad, I can tell you," April smiled at Luke.

"Now it's him I feel sorry for," Luke laughed.

"Yeah, well, don't," April smiled but the bitterness in her voice surprised Luke.

The bell sounded and a voice announced, "Ladies and gentlemen, please take your seats as the second half is about to commence."

Luke, to his surprise, quite enjoyed the second half.

April loved it. She loved the language and the humour and cried at the end.

Luke laughed at her. "It's only pretend," he said in disbelief.

The audience gave the actors a standing ovation.

The play was over at 10.30 and they walked out into a calm March evening.

"Why are you called April if your birthday is in March?" Luke asked. "Why didn't they call you March?"

"Hilarious," April commented. "I must have been asked that very same question about . . . " she pretended to consider, "about one million, two hundred and fifty-six times."

"Nice name – April," Luke said.

There was a silence.

Luke tried again. "Even though I've never heard of the fella that wrote the play, it was good. I really enjoyed myself." He gave a mock bow and said, "Anytime you're stuck for a theatre date in future, I'm your man!"

"Yeah, well, next time be on time," April half smiled at him.

"So there will be a next time?" Luke saw her blush and, not wanting to embarrass her, asked, "Do you wanna go to Supermac's for a burger?"

"That'd be great," April agreed, as she kicked herself for going red.

68

Luke pushed open the door of the fast food restaurant and asked her what she wanted. He bought her a Coke and a pizza and they carried their trays upstairs.

April began to eat and found to her surprise that she was quite hungry. The pizza was delicious. "This is great," she smiled at Luke.

"Yeah, the stuff they do here is nice," he told her. "Don't they have a Supermac's in Cork?"

April shook her head. "Not in Cork city."

"Where do you usually go to eat out?" he asked as he stuffed the remains of his second burger into his mouth.

April shrugged. "Mostly Bewley's."

"Yeah?" Luke said. "God, I'd never think of goin' in there."

"Well, I'd never have thought of coming here."

"That's 'cause you're a culchie," Luke slagged her as he wiped his mouth with the back of his hand and gulped down his Coke. "Are you right? If we don't hurry, we'll end up walkin' to Ballinteer."

"Ready when you are," April answered.

They left the diner and strolled in silence down O'Connell Street. Luke was racking his brains trying to think of something to say. He wanted desperately to impress her. He hated himself for feeling tongue-tied like this.

April was disappointed that the night was coming to an end. She had really enjoyed Luke's company, he was a good laugh and not a bit like everyone said he was.

"Thanks for coming," April eventually said, breaking the silence.

Luke shrugged. "Told you, I didn't mind. I enjoyed myself."

"I'm glad."

The bus arrived and they boarded it. They talked and

laughed all the way home. They liked the same bands, though he had been to concerts and she never had. They liked the same corny jokes, though he was better at telling them than her. He kept pretending to miss the punch-line of her jokes and then he'd say, "God, that's really funny, I promise I'll laugh in a minute."

April walloped him and he began to laugh. "Don't ever become a comedian," he advised as they got off the bus.

"Thanks for the advice."

"What are you goin' to do with your life?" he asked. "Jack says you're a real brain."

April stared at him for a second. Then, turning away, she said softly, "Have you not heard? I'm going to be a doctor."

"Wow!"

"Big wow."

Luke watched her. She didn't seem too happy about it. "Did I say somethin' wrong?" he asked.

"No," she laughed. "I'm fine." She gave him a smile then, a smile that made his heart ache.

He couldn't help it. He reached out and touched her cheek with his fingertips. She didn't pull away.

April could feel her heart beat, beat, beat. She wanted to take his hand in hers. She looked at him and didn't even go red.

Luke still had his hand on her cheek. He didn't want to take it away. Slowly he let his hand drop to his side. "Sorry," he mumbled.

April was surprised at her forwardness. "It was nice," she said softly. A blush flared red on her face. "Don't say sorry."

Luke bit his lip. He shrugged and, without looking at

70

her, said, "I'm no good at sayin' things, April, but I have to tell you, I can't get you out of me head an' if I don't kiss you I'll . . . aw, I dunno." He stopped and shrugged and gazed at her from under his fringe.

April felt so high, so dizzy. This guy, this guy who wasn't afraid of things like she was, was interested in her. She couldn't believe it. But the things he had said tonight . . . and the way he talked to her . . . she felt that she had known him for ages. There was something about him that seemed so familiar.

"I think I'd like you to kiss me," she said, her heart pumping. She hoped that he wouldn't guess that, at seventeen, she had never been kissed.

She knew her parents would freak but, for once, she didn't care.

Luke left April to the door of the Walshes. "See you tomorrow around lunch-time?" he asked. He was delighted when she agreed.

He turned to walk home, his heart heavy and light. What had he done? he wondered. He was mad to want to see her, he told himself. But he couldn't help it. She treated him like a real person. He knew he would have to tell her but he just couldn't tonight. He wanted her to be his girlfriend for just one night at least. He'd tell her tomorrow, he vowed. He'd tell her the reason people thought he was crazy.

Chapter Twelve

"Well?" Sarah demanded, staring at April across the kitchen table. She was munching her fourth slice of toast and waiting expectantly for news.

April bided her time, teasing her. "Well, what?"

"Last night?" Sarah prompted, eyebrows arched. "The play? How did he behave?"

"Last night was fine. We got on fine."

Sarah's face dropped. "You mean you still like him?" She poured herself another cup of tea. "God, he must've been on his best behaviour."

April took a deep breath. This was terrible, especially as she knew how much Sarah disliked Luke. "I still like him," she nodded. Then, with as much nonchalance as she could muster, she said airily, "Actually, he kissed me."

Sarah's teacup met its Maker as it crashed to the floor. The teapot quivered dangerously in her hand. "THE FECKER! GOD! I HOPE YOU TOLD HIM TO GET LOST! GOD! THE NERVE OF THE GUY. GOD!" When April made no reply, she said incredulously, "You did tell him to take a runnin' jump, didn't you?"

"I'm seeing him at lunch-time," April said quietly. She watched as Sarah sank back into the kitchen chair.

"You can't, you just can't," she said. "Honest, April, he's not your type."

72

April was about to reply when the doorbell rang.

"I'll get it," Jack yelled from the hallway. "I think it's for me, anyhow." He opened the door to find Luke standing on the doorstep. "Is there trainin' this mornin'?" Jack asked him, rubbing his eyes blearily.

Luke shook his head.

"What do you want so?" Jack was never at his best in the morning.

"I, eh, I just want a word with April." Luke tried to sound confident.

"April?" Jack stared at him. "Why?"

Luke could feel resentment building inside him. "My business, isn't it?"

Jack bit his lip. He knew that if he said anything there would be a row. "You mind what you tell her," he said in a low, warning voice. "You don't fill her full of crap, do you hear?"

Luke looked him straight in the eye. "What's that supposed to mean?"

"I know you, Coleman," Jack was not attempting to be friendly now. "You're mad after her. I'm tellin' you not to upset her life here. She doesn't need you."

Luke shifted from one foot to the other. He didn't want a fight. "Thanks for the advice," he tried to say in as pleasant a voice as he could. "Now will you get April for me?"

Jack turned abruptly from him and marched into the kitchen. He found April and Sarah sitting staring at each other in silence. "Visitor for you." Jack looked at April. "Your friend from last night."

Sarah gawped. "Luke?"

April fled out of the kitchen, mortified, but she could hear Sarah exclaiming, "Dad'll go spare."

"You said lunch-time. People don't usually eat lunch

at eleven o'clock in the morning," April said in amusement as she met Luke at the front door.

Luke looked up and shrugged. "I know I said lunchtime, but I need to tell you somethin' and it couldn't wait – can you come for a walk?"

"What is it?" April asked. He looked dishevelled, as if he hadn't slept. "Will you come in? Do you want a cuppa? You look awful."

"I'd prefer a walk."

April got her coat, told Jack and Sarah where she was going and, without waiting to hear the questions that she knew Sarah was dying to ask, left the house pulling Luke in her wake.

He said nothing until they reached Marlay Park. April wondered what the story was – he seemed in a bad mood. "OK," she said, dreading what she was going to hear. "What is it?" She tried to laugh. "Just tell me and then I can go home and finish my breakfast."

Luke sat down on a bench and April sat beside him. There was a brief silence and then Luke turned to her. "Have you heard any stories about me?"

April didn't know what to say. There was no point in getting Sarah and Jack into trouble. "No, not really," she lied.

"Warnings to keep away?"

April shrugged. "Not exactly warnings."

Luke stared out into the distance. He stared at the huge house that dominated the park and at the woods beyond it. He wished that he was anywhere but here, trying to explain to a girl that he really liked, that he had only last night kissed, why she was better off without him. He swallowed hard. He'd promised himself that he'd tell her the truth. "If I don't tell you, someone else will," he began. "I want to tell you from my point of view, 'cause it was me that was involved, not flippin' Jack or Sarah or anyone else."

April shrugged. She didn't want to hear anything bad. "Look," she faltered, "what happened in the past shouldn't matter. You're still you, and I like you. I don't really care what anyone says . . . "

"That's easy to say now," Luke interrupted. He paused, then continued, "I'm surprised you haven't heard before now. No one really talks about me; I guess they're, I dunno, afraid of me or somethin'." He looked April in the eyes. "I want to tell you, I want you to hear my side of things." God, he hated this. "Do you remember when you heard I got expelled from school?"

April nodded.

"Well, I kinda lied. I was rude and disruptive an' all the stuff I said, but the thing that got me expelled was different." He stopped and grinned. "I'd never've been expelled otherwise, 'cause I was the school football team. Just me – no one else. They wouldn't've let me go." His grin vanished. "I was in science class one Monday mornin' an' I was fed up. I nicked the teacher's keys from his desk an' after class I went out an' started his car up. I was planning to take her drivin' up the mountains," Luke faltered as he heard April's intake of breath. "I was takin' her for a drive. She was a beaut. Anyhow, some of the lads see me an' they feckin' jumped in the back. I told 'em to feck off but they wouldn't an' so I reckoned that I'd scare them, shake them up, so I take off an' drove like a flippin' lunatic." Luke's voice went quiet as he remembered. "They were lovin' every second of it – Crazy Coleman livin' up to his name. Anyhow," Luke looked directly at April, "I lost control of the car, we flipped over an' over an' the car was a write-off." He shrugged. "Two of the lads ended up in hospital for weeks, they could've died; all my bleedin' fault. I was hauled up in court, got a suspended sentence, got expelled, got beaten up by the brothers of one of the lads, got a crummy job with me ma's help an' that's it." He was afraid to look at her.

April felt shocked. "Why?" she whispered.

The question startled him. He stared at her, puzzled. "Why wha'?"

"Why did you take the car?"

"Told you," Luke snapped. "I was pissed off."

April looked at him in disbelief. "I get like that," she said. "I don't go out and rob a car."

Luke turned away and said nothing.

"There must've been some reason," she persisted. "Did it make you feel good or something? How did you feel?"

He gave an exasperated shrug. "Dunno." Then he paused. "There's a song that kinda describes it," he began slowly. "It was playin' in the car and afterwards I went an' bought the tape. I guess that's how I felt. Drunk. Drunk an' powerful an', an', I dunno," he searched for the right expression, "in control, I guess." He stared at her. "The point is, April, I took the bleedin' car."

"What's the song?"

Luke stared at her. Was anything he said going in? "It's a Tracy Chapman song," he answered, "*Fast Car*."

"I know it," April nodded. "It's a great song."

"Yeah." Luke took April's hands in his. "You know now what kinda person I am. I've always been a little bit crazy. I won't change, at least I don't think I can. I won't blame you if you don't want to see me any more."

April's mind reeled. Everyone deserved a chance. You couldn't just write people off . . . "They got into the

76

car themselves, you didn't force them. It's not your fault, Luke."

Luke sighed. "In court they told everyone that they'd begged me to stop – they bleedin' well lied! One of them was a fella Sarah went out with. She blamed me for everythin'."

There was a silence. April looked at him, he wouldn't meet her eyes. He looked dejected. Her mind was spinning. Her head told her that he must be mad. But her heart went out to him. She knew there had to be some good in him; why else had he told her?

"What other crazy things have you done?" April asked.

Luke's head jerked up and he looked at her sharply.

April didn't know whether she was doing the right thing or not, by asking, but it felt right. "If I'm to go out with you, I might as well know all the dirt."

"What I've just told you, it doesn't put you off me?"

"No," April stated simply. "I know people will say I'm stupid but, no, I think you're interesting."

"You serious?"

"Yeah." April smiled.

"You're crazier than I ever was." Luke smiled at her in admiration. She wasn't afraid. He felt as if a huge weight had been lifted from his shoulders. He'd been awake all night trying to figure out a way to tell her. "Crazy things I've done . . . " he grinned. "Where d'you want me to start? I've run away from home, twice," he began. "I used to steal money from me oul' fella. Now, that was good." April watched a smile spread over his face. "That was good," he repeated.

They sat for an hour in the park. Luke talked and she listened. Some of his stories were funny, some outrageous, some frightening. When April asked why he had done such mad things, Luke just shrugged. "Dunno," he answered, or "I just wanted to."

Eventually Luke asked, "What about you? I'll bet you've stories of your own." He looked at her expectantly.

April stopped smiling. "No, none."

"Aw, come on," Luke coaxed. "I'll bet you've loadsa dirt to spill."

"No!"

Luke was startled. "Sorry," he mumbled. "I wasn't suggestin' that you were like me or anythin'."

"I know that," April was kneading her hands. "I didn't mean to snap at you," She tried to smile. "I'm just a boring storyteller."

It was a feeble excuse but he let her away with it. "I second that," he joked and he was rewarded with a laugh. "So," he asked in an attempt to keep her talking, "why a doctor?"

"Huh?"

"Why do you want to be a doctor?" He shrugged. "Like, did you see some doc do wonderful things and decide 'yeah, I want this'?"

"My dad's a doctor."

Luke laughed. "Yeah, well, my oul' fella's a night watchman on a building site up the road; don't mean I wanna be one."

April said nothing.

"So why else?" Luke asked. "Do you think yer da's great?"

"Do you have to ask so many questions?" April glared at him. "I don't analyse everything I want." She stopped abruptly. Her eyes filled with tears and Luke froze. He hoped she wasn't going to cry. He couldn't handle tears.

April blinked rapidly. She shook her head as if she were clearing it. "Sorry," she whispered. "Sorry."

Luke gulped. "Did I say somethin'? What did I say?"

"Nothing," April shook her head. "It's just me. I don't like thinking about the future, you know."

"Some great future you'll have," Luke nudged her affectionately. "Bleedin' doctors are loaded."

"I don't want to be a doctor," April said quietly. The confession almost made her dizzy. "I can't stand even thinking about it, much less discussing it." She gave a small shrug. "I've never said that to anyone before."

"Why on earth . . . ?"

"My dad, my mum. I wanted to do medicine once; now, it's all they talk about. I can't let them down."

Luke looked at her as if she were mad. "That's crap," he said. "If they love you at all, they'll let you do what you want."

"I love them," April whispered. "I don't want to let them down."

Luke felt angry. "They're lettin' you down," he insisted. He grabbed her by the shoulders and the intensity in his voice startled her. "Do what *you* want, April, for Christ's sake."

"I'm not like you," April removed his hands from her shoulders. "I don't just do what I want – I consider other people."

Luke felt as if she had slapped him. He wanted to tell her that he didn't do just what he wanted, but he couldn't. Instead he shrugged. "Fair enough."

After a small silence, he asked, "What would you do, if you had a choice?"

April wrapped her arms around herself and stared into the distance. "Paint," she said softly. "I'd paint."

"Wha'?" Luke grinned. "Paint bleedin' houses!"

"No, dope," April rolled her eyes. "Pictures. Cartoons. I'd be a female Gary Larson."

"You'd have to be funny, though," Luke was delighted to see her smile. "You are one sad person, you'd never be like Larson."

She tried to belt him but missed.

Grabbing hold of her hand, he hauled her up from the seat. "Do you want to go to McDonald's for breakfast, seein' as I spoilt your other one?" He fumbled in his jeans and dragged out a ragged fiver. "Ya can get an Egg McMuffin or somethin'."

"Sounds delicious," April slagged. Then she said softly, "Please don't tell anyone about me not wanting to do medicine."

Luke laughed. He spread his arms wide. "Sure who'd I tell?" he joked. "No one talks to me 'cept you."

April began to laugh.

Luke grinned and, putting his arm around her shoulder, he pulled her close. "So?" he asked. "McDonald's?"

"Yeah, but I insist you have the Egg McMuffin. I'll stick to tea."

"Somehow I feel that generosity isn't behind that suggestion," Luke grinned. "But it just so happens I love them egg things."

He ignored the puking sounds April made.

Chapter Thirteen

"Good weekend?" Jimmy glanced at Coleman out of the corner of his eye.

Luke was reading the paper with his feet plonked on top of the dash. "Seein' as I never got paid on Friday I guess it was all right." Jimmy never paid him on time.

Jimmy rolled his eyes. "Yeah, sorry 'bout that." He fumbled in his pocket and pulled out Luke's pay-packet. "Here, better late then never."

Luke took it and grinned.

"So," Jimmy asked again, "Good weekend?"

"It was all right. I went to a play."

"Yeah." Jimmy laughed. It wasn't much of a joke, but the lad was trying.

"Naw, serious, I did. *The Last Christian Steward* by your man, Roddy Doyle."

"Yeah?"

"It was good," Luke nodded. "I liked it, anyhow."

Jimmy licked his lips. There was information waiting to be found here. "Who'd you go with?"

"I went with me girlfriend," Luke said as casually as he could. He enjoyed Jimmy's look of disbelief which was quickly replaced by encouragement and then, with a warning look on his face, Jimmy wagged his finger saying, "Don't let her trap you. Women all want the one thing – a man, a house and a kid. Look what happened to me – don't make the same mistakes."

Luke solemnly shook his head. "Naw, I'll never make the mistakes you did, Jim."

Jimmy looked at him sharply. Was the kid being smart?

Luke looked back innocently.

"Tell us more about this girl," Jimmy urged.

Sarah was astounded. "April, you can't go out with him. Your folks will go spare." She slammed the front door and the two began the walk to school.

April laughed. "Sure, why would they do that? They don't even know Luke." She made a dismissive gesture.

"*You* don't know Luke." Sarah looked beseechingly at her. "Please, April, he's mad. You don't know him well enough. He's good-lookin', I'll give him that, but he's crazy. He's done some mad things. Please, April, don't get involved."

April was touched that Sarah seemed to care so much. She smiled and said gently, "Sarah, he's told me all the things he's done. I still like him."

"About the car? Mr Boyle's car? Has he told you that?" Sarah demanded.

"Yeah."

"About the lads he nearly killed?"

"It wasn't all his fault. They were as thick as he was."

"No one is as thick as Luke."

April said nothing. There was no point. Sarah had her mind made up about Luke and there was no way she would change it. Instead, she said quietly, "Everyone is all right when you bother to get to know them."

"Yeah, sure." April was too soft, Sarah thought glumly. Luke was just taking advantage of her. "I'm sorry I'm not glad for you," she eventually said. "I can't help it. I know Luke a lot longer than you and he's always been trouble. I just don't want you to end up hurt."

April could feel tears behind her eyes. Sarah didn't want her to be hurt. That must be a first. "Thanks," she said shakily. "But I won't be hurt, I know I won't."

Sarah thought of the way her da had reacted when Jack told him that April was seeing Luke. He had gone mental. He wanted to put a stop to it there and then, but her ma had restrained him. "If we do that," she had said, "it will only make him even more attractive to her. Leave it for the moment and see what happens."

Sarah had glared at her mother. "I can't believe you," she had raged. "He's totally unreliable. You would rather he hurt her than do anything to stop it. Well, you won't stop me sayin' what I think!"

"I doubt anyone would stop you," Jack had said sardonically and she had flung a cushion at him. The debate had finished in uproar.

"See you later," April broke into Sarah's thoughts. They had reached the school building and both were going to different classes.

"Yeah, see you later," Sarah answered.

Jimmy was getting decidedly restless. Luke was talking on and on about this play he had gone to. The plot sounded like a load of crap. Jimmy yawned to give the hint that he was getting a bit fed up.

Luke grinned to himself. He was boring Jimmy senseless and it was great. He thought of all the mornings that Jimmy had done the same to him. Feeling a bit remorseful, Luke asked, "OK, Jim, how was your weekend?"

And Jimmy was off. He didn't need to be asked twice. "The flippin' wife ruined it," he moaned. "As for that kid . . ."

Luke sighed and shut his mind to Jimmy's whinging. He thought about April and wondered what she was doing right that minute.

April held her breath. Her heart began to pound madly. Mr Kavanagh, biology teacher and madman was advancing upon her. In his hand he held her copy. She knew it was hers because she had spent about an hour writing and decorating her name on its cover. The letters blazed: vivid greens, oranges and blues. As Mr Kavanagh stood over her desk, April tried to look unconcerned.

He threw the book down in front of her and snarled, "That test was a disgrace." If he expected April to reply, he was disappointed. April knew it had been a disgrace, because she hadn't studied for it. She had been out with Sarah and Jack nearly every night last week. The biology test was the last thing on her mind. She was weeks behind in her father's carefully-worked-out study programme. She wasn't due to study the worm for another two months.

"Well?" Mr Kavanagh demanded, gazing down on April. "Any excuse?"

April licked her lips. This was the first test she had ever failed and she couldn't believe that she didn't even feel upset. "I study my books chapter by chapter," April haltingly explained. "You seem to jump from chapter to chapter and it doesn't fit in with my plan."

The class exploded with laughter. April looked around in surprise – she hadn't meant to be funny.

Mr Kavanagh narrowed his eyes. "So, when will you

be studying the worm?" he asked, his voice dangerously sarcastic.

April, who wasn't yet used to the teacher's moods, considered the question seriously. "In another six weeks or so," she answered.

"So I'll give you the test in six weeks' time, shall I?" Mr Kavanagh had folded his arms, another bad sign.

April was confused. She didn't know if an answer was expected. Eventually, as the silence stretched onward, she nodded. "Fine," she agreed.

There was more loud laughter. Mr Kavanagh was fuming. The nerve of this young one! "How dare you!" he said, his voice shaking with rage. "How dare you be so cheeky."

"I only answered your question," April defended herself. She was confused. "I wasn't being smart, I really wasn't."

"Detention." Mr Kavanagh stalked back up the class, leaving April open-mouthed. He took the register up and wrote her name on it for disobedience. "Detention till six all next week."

"That's not fair," April was surprised to hear herself argue back. "I only answered your question." She glared at her teacher. "

"Detention for the next two weeks," Mr Kavanagh said calmly. "And you can resit that test and, if you don't get at least ninety per cent in it, detention for three weeks."

April felt as if something inside her snapped. She was not going to be bullied by anyone. "I won't do it." She picked up her bag and books and said, "I won't do detention."

There was a horrified silence.

Mr Kavanagh folded his arms. "Really?"

April nodded. "Really."

"Then get out of my class," the teacher roared. "I'll not have you in this class a moment longer. Your work is terrible and has been since you came; your attitude today is shameful." His face had gone purple. He wagged a finger in her direction. "I'll be having a word with your tutor over this."

April took her coat down from the coat-hanger. She nodded up at him. "Fine," she said, with as much composure as she could muster. "Do that." She walked to the door. The silence in the room was complete, the tension just about to bubble over. Gently she opened the door and walked out. Her head was high, her eyes blazing, and she felt in control for the first time in her life.

Luke hopped out to unload the van as Jimmy parked in front of the shop.

God, he thought. Am I bleedin' glad to get out of there. There was only so much a guy could take of Jimmy. He wondered how his family could stand him – by all accounts, they couldn't, and the feeling was reciprocated by Jimmy. He had referred to his wife as "an oul' bag" forty times in two hours. Luke had amused himself by counting. When Jimmy asked what he was smiling at, Luke had grinned, saying, "Aw, you've a way with words, Jim." Jimmy had preened himself, announcing that he was always a good storyteller.

"Hiya, lads," Mary, the owner of the shop, came out to greet them. She began to slag Jimmy about not giving Luke a hand.

"I stayed in here so I could be the one to see your gorgeous face first," Jimmy replied, leering at her.

Luke made puking noises and they both laughed.

"This fella has a mot," Jimmy thumbed to Luke, who raised his eyes heavenwards. "I'm tellin' you," he addressed Luke then, "you'll have to be practising the nice lines for her. Take a lesson off your Uncle Jim."

"Who's the girl?" Mary came around to the back, agog with interest.

"Will you get lost," Luke said. He lifted some food from the back of the van, went into the shop and deposited it on the counter. He pretended not to hear them both laughing.

Jimmy came in behind him then, obviously deciding to help out with the rest of the order.

Mary signed her bill and waved them off. "Give my best to the girlfriend," she yelled.

"There's a fine woman," Jimmy said as he hooted the horn.

Luke laughed and Jimmy looked at him in surprise.

"Every woman is fine to you," Luke grinned. "It's the ones you marry you don't seem to like."

Jimmy slapped Luke on the back. "That's me boy, you're coppin' on," he praised. Privately, he thought, I hope he keeps going out with this young wan, she must have some effect on him – laughin' on a Monday – bleedin' laughin' at all!

April felt high. Everyone was telling her how well she had handled Kavanagh. It was all over the school at this stage – a fifth year had given Mr Kavanagh the two fingers. She hadn't meant it to be a big deal, April tried to explain, she had just thought he was being unfair. It's important to stand up for yourself, April said. Everyone agreed with her. Stand up to the injustice of teachers.

April was the most-sought after girl that day,

everyone wanted a piece of her. It was great. Sarah wanted a blow-by-blow account of the incident. April found it hard to remember all the details but everyone else could. They said that April had actually said, "You can kiss my ass if you want me back in your class."

At two o'clock, during maths class, a note came for April. She was to see her form tutor. Mr Ryan, the maths teacher, breathed a sigh of relief when she left. The girl who had been so quiet was actually attempting to disrupt his class. Well, she wasn't actually causing any trouble, but the others were. They all kept looking to her for approval and April would smile in that half-embarrassed way of hers and say nothing. Mr Ryan knew what had happened in Colm Kavanagh's class. He knew that there had been more trouble in Colm's class after the Gavin girl had walked out. He shook his head in disbelief – she had seemed so well-balanced and quiet.

"Good luck," people whispered as April walked past them out of class. She grinned back and tried to let on she wasn't bothered. She felt like puking. She knew she was in deep trouble but she also knew she had only done what she thought was right.

Knocking on her tutor's door, she was told to come in.

Miss Allen was sitting at her desk, a pile of copies beside her. She looked up as April entered. She nodded to a chair and April sat down. "What happened in biology today?" she asked in a clipped voice.

April told her as much as she could remember. She attempted to look guilty, even sorry, but she couldn't. She felt proud of what she had done. She felt proud of herself.

There was a silence when April finished her story. Miss Allen let the silence do its work on the girl. April became fidgety, restless. "Did you tell other students to walk out of his class?" she inquired briskly.

April jumped and reddened. "No."

"Did you say that everyone should stand together against injustice?"

April could have fainted in fear. "Well, not exactly . . ." she stammered. "I, I said . . ."

"Yes?"

"I said everyone should stand up for themselves, but I said that at lunch-time . . ."

"Oh, did you now?" Miss Allen studied this girl, who in the space of a day had caused outright mutiny in all of Mr Kavanagh's classes. People were walking out everywhere. Of course she knew that Colm could be a bit heavy-handed, but what was happening was ridiculous. She leaned over towards April. "I want you to apologise to Mr Kavanagh," she said. "I want you to ask to be allowed back into his class."

April swallowed and slowly shook her head. "I can't do that," she said finally. "He asked me a question, I didn't know he thought I was being cheeky."

"You will say sorry."

April shook her head. "No, I won't. I can't." April knew that, if she gave in, something precious that she had done today would be lost. "I'm sorry, Miss Allen, but I can't."

"I've talked to Mr Kavanagh," Miss Allen ignored April's last statement. "His story is similar to yours. He says you failed a biology test very badly and didn't seem a bit concerned. Is that true?"

April shrugged. This was a nightmare. "I never studied for the test." She bit her lip. "I haven't got to that chapter in my study plan yet. I never usually fail tests, it's not as if I did it on purpose."

"You were cheeky when asked why you had failed." Miss Allen was counting April's misdemeanours on her fingers. "You told him that he was being unfair when he gave you detention and then you announced that you wouldn't do it." She paused. "Now, who would you say is at fault?"

April felt tears well up in her eyes, tears of frustration and anger. "He, he . . ." she gulped, "he was being sarcastic and I didn't know. He told everyone that my work was a disgrace. He shouldn't have said that in front of everyone." She gasped for breath. "I wasn't being cheeky or smart, it's not my fault he thought so."

Miss Allen passed her a tissue. "Calm down," she said gently. "Don't upset yourself."

"And I didn't tell everyone to walk out of his classes, either," April said with spirit. "No one likes him."

"I'm not here to discuss what the students think of a teacher," Miss Allen said sharply. "I am ordering you to apologise to Mr Kavanagh."

April stared at her mutinously.

"If you don't apologise, you won't be allowed into the biology class and, furthermore, you could face suspension." She leaned back in her seat. "Now, what'll it be?"

April felt as if her world were crumbling. She, April Gavin, suspended from school. She shook her head. "I can't," she whispered. "I just can't."

"Is that your final word?" Miss Allen felt upset. She didn't know why the girl was being so stubborn. "Are you sure you won't say sorry?"

April thought she was going to be sick. She looked down at her hands and said nothing.

"All right," the teacher sighed. "I hate doing this, but as from now you are suspended from biology for as long as Mr Kavanagh and the principal feel it necessary. You will go to the library to study during biology classes and do any work assigned to you." She gazed at April's bent head. "I'll also be writing to your parents or, in your case, your guardians to inform them of what has happened."

April gave a shaky sigh. At least it was only the Walshes who would know. "Fine," she muttered.

"Now get out of my sight," Miss Allen ordered. "You are a very foolish girl."

April ran out of the room and into the Ladies'. She locked herself in a cubicle, sat down on the toilet and cried. She felt defeated but also strangely elated, as if she had gained something far more important by rebelling than by smoothing things over, as she had done the whole of her life.

Jimmy dropped Luke at the end of his road, and with a "bip" of his horn he drove off. When Jimmy was out of sight, Luke took thirty pounds out of his wages and stuck it, together with his wage slip, in his shoe. Then, assuming a jaunty walk, he made his way home.

His da was waiting at the door. He let Luke in and held out his hand. Luke, with a sullen look, handed over his wages. His da counted it, moaning about how little he was earning, took sixty out and handed his son back the remaining twenty pounds.

"New wheels for the car," he sneered, then pushing past his son, Mr Coleman left the house, slamming the door.

"Creep," Luke muttered as he went into the kitchen to find his mother.

She smiled and told him to sit down. "He take your

money again?" she asked, putting a plate of stew in front of him.

"Not all of it." Luke managed a grin. He pulled off his shoe and pressed the thirty pounds into her hands. This was a ritual that happened every week. "Take it, Ma," he urged. "I've still got twenty. Get yourself somethin', get Davy somethin' – I don't need it."

His mother resisted. "No, Luke, you earned it. Just this once, spend some on yourself."

Luke shook his head. "You earn it too, you know," he said seriously. "Please, Ma, I'd feel better."

Mrs Coleman ruffled his hair and blinked away her tears. "What would I do without you?" she whispered and pocketed the cash.

"It's him," Sarah said, handing the phone receiver to April. She said "him" with such distaste, April knew it was Luke on the phone.

"Thanks," she said sweetly as Sarah flounced into the kitchen.

"Hi, Luke?"

"Eh, hi," Luke replied. "I, eh, just thought I'd ring you."

"That was a nice thought," April smiled into the phone.

"Yeah, yeah, it was, wasn't it?" Luke joked. "Me mind doesn't know what's happened. Havin' a nice thought is a kinda rare experience for it."

"Having any thoughts at all is pretty rare for your mind, I'd say," April teased.

"Now that's nasty," Luke failed miserably at trying to sound hurt. When April stopped giggling, he asked, "How'd your day go?"

"I've had better," April sighed. "I've had a lot better."

"Yeah? How come?"

"Kavanagh threw me out of his class," April said in a whisper. She was afraid to talk any louder in case Mr or Mrs Walsh would hear.

"Kavanagh?" Luke sounded puzzled. "Not biology Kavanagh?"

"The very same," April confirmed.

"Wow," Luke whistled. "What did you do?"

April told him in frantic whispers, terrified Mr Walsh would decide to come into the hall. Luke was almost crying with laughter by the end of her story. April began to laugh as well.

"So," Luke asked, becoming serious again, "What now, you gonna say sorry?"

"No, I'm not," April said indignantly. "It's a matter of principle. He can whistle for his apology."

Luke rejoiced when he heard that. He knew she wasn't afraid, she could face anything.

"Good for you," he said solemnly, "You stick to your guns."

April felt her confidence rise another notch. Luke was proud of her, she could tell from his voice. She knew she was right. "I intend to," she grinned.

"It might get rough, though." Luke warned her.

"I've been through worse," April said quietly, almost to herself.

"Sorry?"

"Nothing," April hastily changed the subject. "So, how'd your day go?"

"I spent it with Jimmy," Luke replied, laughing, "How do you think it went?"

Chapter Fourteen

The letter from school arrived. Sarah spied it sitting on the windowsill when they arrived in from school.

She opened it and grinned at April. "I think you'll be all right until after the weekend, anyhow," she whispered. She stopped abruptly as her mother began to descend the stairway. "It only says they want to see Ma and Da in order to discuss your progress in school." Sarah scanned the brief letter again. "Next Monday," she nodded. "The shit should hit the fan on Monday."

April couldn't help but smile. "Thanks a bunch for that consoling thought," she grinned.

Sarah put the letter back where she had found it. "You shoulda seen Kavanagh's class yesterday," she grinned. Sarah had him for pass biology. "If Kavanagh asked a question and someone got it right, everyone would yell 'fair dues' and 'fair play' an' all. It was funny. The word 'fair' was the most used word in the class."

April smiled. She never thought that her action would incite such excitement among the students. Kavanagh had been the most feared and most hated teacher in the school; now he was a laughing-stock. She hadn't meant that to happen. Everyone was on her side, everyone knew her. People had even offered to help do the extra work she had got lumbered with in study hall.

Jack and Sarah were behind her all the way, though Jack had advised her to apologise because he'd told her that his da would throw a wobbler when he found out. "The time I got into trouble in school he went mental," he'd said.

But she'd refused.

Luke had even been on at her to say sorry. "Oh, yeah, like you were a model student," she'd laughed. And he'd grinned broadly and shrugged. "Guess I can't talk," he'd said. Then he'd kissed her and told her that she had guts and her heart had soared. She was mad about him.

"People up here are gas," April mused aloud.

Sarah stared at her. "People are much the same everywhere," she answered.

April wondered if that was true. She knew she wasn't the same.

Jack and Sarah were yelling at each other. Sarah had flatly refused to dry the dinner dishes.

"It's not fair, Ma," she fumed, appealing to her mother. "He always gets out of cleanin' the kitchen."

Jack grinned. "Not true, sis," he waved a finger at her face. "I've got football trainin' tonight, so I can't do the dishes." He looked longingly at the draining-board and said mournfully, "I'd bring them with me an' dry them if I could." He grinned at his mother. "You know I would, Ma."

April bit her lip to stop from laughing. She had got used to these brother-sister rows. Jack usually managed to come out on top as Sarah was too fiery to make much sense half the time.

"GET OUT!" Sarah hit Jack with the wet dish-cloth, leaving a red mark down one side of his face.

"Sarah!" Mrs Walsh began to berate her daughter and Jack slipped out.

April was still smiling when Mr Walsh appeared at the kitchen door. He looked nervous and on edge. He beckoned to April. "Can I have a word?"

April followed him into the front room of the house, aware that Mrs Walsh and Sarah had gone silent behind her. She knew it was about the letter. She wondered what he would say. Mr Walsh closed the dining-room door and asked April to sit down. He swallowed, sat down himself and pulled the letter from his shirt pocket. "I got this from the school today," he announced.

April could feel her mouth go dry. She tried to look innocent. "Yes?"

"It says here," Mr Walsh put on his glasses and began to read directly from the letter, "your presence is required to discuss April's progress in school to date. Please be in my office on Monday 26th at 4.15 pm." Glancing at April he asked, "Do you know what this is all about?"

April shrugged. "Is it because I'm a new student?"

Mr Walsh's face began to glow with something akin to relief. He nodded. "It could be," he muttered, "I never considered that." He smiled; his smile was definitely one of relief. "I thought for a moment that you were in trouble. Jack got one of these years ago," he indicated the letter. "Turned out he was the class clown." He smiled at April. "You'd never behave like that, I was stupid to even think so."

April wondered if her face was red. She felt like a total heel. "I wouldn't say I was a clown," she began haltingly and then, when Mr Walsh looked up sharply, her courage deserted her. "No, I'm definitely not a clown." She got up to leave. She would face the music next Monday. Besides getting thrown out of biology, her other work had slipped as well.

It wasn't surprising – she had a life now.

Mr Walsh studied April. He liked her enormously. She wasn't the docile egghead he'd expected, Jack and Sarah hadn't become more studious as a result of her presence, but still, he liked her.

"Can I go now, Mr Walsh?" April broke into his reverie. "I think I'd better help Sarah with the dishes."

"You seeing that Luke fella tonight?" he asked. Now it was his turn to go red. The question obviously made him uncomfortable; it was the first time he had asked her directly about Luke.

April looked at her feet. "Eh, yeah," she nodded. "I'm meeting him after his football practice."

"Oh, he's going to that, is he?" Mr Walsh nodded in approval. "That's good, he's a good player." He looked April in the eye. "I know it's none of my business," he began to look away now, "but you've seen him every night this week. I hear you're, you know, doing a line."

April blushed. My God, she thought, what is he at? "Only since last Saturday," she gulped.

"Yeah, well, he's a wild card." Mr Walsh patted her on the shoulder as he went by her out of the room. "Just don't get too involved, all right."

April felt stunned. Did parents always do this? Discuss things? It felt nice. It felt safe. As if he kinda cared.

Chapter Fifteen

April tensed as the bedroom door closed. She didn't turn to see who had come in; instead she bent further over her art history essay and waited for the person to speak. To her relief it was Mrs Walsh. "April, Dan and I went down to see your tutor today."

April turned around in her chair. "Now you know," she said simply.

Mrs Walsh nodded. She had managed to persuade her husband to let her deal with April. He had been furious while she had been shocked. "What's happened?" she asked. "Miss Allen says the school in Cork gave you a great report."

April said nothing.

"Then, up here," Mrs Walsh continued, "your work flops. Why, April?" Without waiting for an answer, she went on, "And that story of you fighting with the biology teacher, I can't believe it."

"He was unfair," April said. "I wasn't being cheeky." She looked beseechingly at Mrs Walsh. "Please, you've got to believe me."

"April, you have got to apologise."

April hung her head and looked at her hands. "No."

"They'll suspend you from school," Mrs Walsh said

desperately. Then, seeing she was getting nowhere, added, "Miss Allen is very worried about you."

"Why? I'm fine."

Mrs Walsh pressed her hands together and looked hard at this girl whom she tried to treat as another daughter. April was difficult to know. Sarah was mad about her and Jack thought she was a good laugh. The Gavins had led her and Dan to believe that she was a serious, steady girl. "She's worried because your work has gone downhill since you came here, she thinks there has to be a reason for it."

"No reason," April replied, trying to keep her voice light. "I can't keep up with all the study."

Mrs Walsh sighed. It wasn't as if April didn't do any work, she did a lot more than most girls in fifth year. She reached out and touched April on the arm. She hoped the contact would break the barrier she knew was there. "But your other school reports are brilliant. Your father . . ."

"My father hasn't a clue."

Mrs Walsh winced at the bitterness in April's voice. When she looked at April, however, she was smiling.

"He's just so proud of me, I guess he exaggerates when he talks about me." She gave an embarrassed shrug.

"Do you miss your parents?" Miss Allen had told them to ask that. She thought it might be a reason.

"I miss them a bit, but that's not the reason I'm falling behind, honest."

She looked sincere. Mary Walsh took a deep breath. She and Dan had thought of another possibility – this was going to be sensitive. "It's not Luke, is it?"

Now April really looked surprised. "Luke?"

"Well, you're not doing badly just to . . . just to . . . impress him, are you?" The last part came out in a rush.

April was astounded. "That wouldn't impress Luke," she said, as if Mrs Walsh was thick. "How would that impress him?"

"You're right, it wouldn't." Mrs Walsh was almost disappointed. It would have been so easy to blame the lad. She shrugged. "Sorry, April, I had to ask." Then she said, "You've seen him a lot recently, I mean . . ."

"I only see him when I've all my work done," April said firmly. She shrugged. "I don't know what the fuss is about, I'm just getting Bs instead of As. It's not as if it's a major disaster."

"Your As were in the 90% bracket," Mrs Walsh said, copying what the tutor had said to them. "Your Bs are in the low 70s. That's a drop of 20%." She gazed at April and went on, "And then you get thrown out of biology . . ."

April said nothing.

Mrs Walsh then asked, as gently as she could, "Are you sure there's nothing the matter? I can't believe what your tutor told us, Mr Kavanagh throwing you out of the biology class and everything, it just doesn't add up to what your dad told us about you."

April remained silent. How could she tell this woman anything? How could she tell anyone the whole truth about Cork? How could she say how she felt when no one had ever asked her before?

"If something was the matter, you would tell me, wouldn't you?"

April nodded; she couldn't speak.

Mrs Walsh saw April's eyes glisten. "You seem happy here," she continued, hoping April would crack.

"I am happy here," April whispered. "I love it here, I do, really."

"Well, what's the problem?"

No answer.

"April?"

No answer. There was only one thing left for her to do, the girl needed someone to talk to.

"Luke!"

The word was spat out, almost as if the name had left a dirty taste in the speaker's mouth.

Luke jumped up from the floor where he had been watching football on the telly. His heart began to hammer and he took deep breaths to slow it down. His da could smell fear. "Yeah?" Luke answered, trying to sound casual.

"GET OUT HERE!"

Luke walked into the kitchen. He saw his ma cowering on a chair in the corner and Davy, his little brother, had his head buried in her lap. His da dominated the scene. His massive bulk seemed to obscure the light from the window. In his hand he held a piece of paper. Luke took one look at it and his heart began to skip in his chest.

"What's this?" His da waved the paper in front of his nose. He spoke in that awfully polite high tone he used when he got really angry.

Luke shrugged. "Dunno."

"Oh, don't you?" His da shoved it in his face. "Now do you recognise it?"

"It's me payslip from work." Luke winced as his da caught him at the neck. His ma gasped and closed her eyes.

"And how much does it say you earn?" He took Luke over to the kitchen wall and banged his head against it. "How much?"

"A hundred an' ten," Luke gasped.

"How much?" He banged his head a second time.

"A hundred an' ten."

"How come I only ever saw eighty?"

Luke was seeing stars. He tried to stay standing. "I kept some."

His head was banged again. "Where is it?"

"Gone, I spent it all," Luke spat back in a fit of bravado. He saw his ma about to rise and something in his look warned her to sit back down.

An almighty whack sent him sliding to the ground.

"Hello, Mary," Mr Gavin's voice boomed down the line. "How are you? Anything wrong?"

Mrs Walsh drew a nervous breath. She was sure they were doing the right thing. She had talked it over with Dan and it seemed the only course of action. They both agreed that they did not want to be held responsible for April's falling grades. "Not exactly, Jim," she began. "It's about April."

"Oh, my God." His voice held a note of panic. "Is she all right?" In the background, Mrs Walsh heard April's mother exclaim, "What, what is it, Jim?"

"Please, is she OK?" Mr Gavin asked.

"She's fine, health-wise. It's just that she seems to be having a few problems in school." She went on to explain the situation. "The fact is, April will be suspended if she doesn't apologise to this teacher. Her other work isn't as good as it was in Cork, either."

When she finished, there was a stunned silence on the other end of the line. "Jim, are you still there?" she ventured.

His voice, when it came, sounded shocked. "That's impossible. April would never carry on like that. I've never known her to get angry." Then, in a horrified voice, he added, "She can't drop out of biology, she's going to be a doctor, for God's sake."

"She says she can't keep up with the study," Mrs Walsh replied.

Jim Gavin took a deep breath. "I know my daughter, Mary," he began. "She's so clever, she's good enough to do anything. I'm not just boasting, I swear." He turned to his wife and relayed the conversation to her.

Mrs Gavin came on the line. "Hi, Mary. Are you sure April is all right, healthy, I mean, because this doesn't sound like her. I don't think she's ever been in trouble in school in her life."

"I wish I could say the same about my two," Mrs Walsh joked. When this was received by silence, she again said that April seemed perfectly healthy. She cursed her husband for chickening out of this call. He had assured her that she would be better at it. A woman knows the right things to say, he had proclaimed. "Her tutor wondered if she was missing you both," Mrs Walsh ventured. "She thought that that could cause her work to slip."

"Do you think she is?"

"I can't say. She doesn't seem to be, but it could be an act. I questioned her about things and, I hate to say this, but I have a gut feeling that she's keeping something back."

"Like what?"

"I don't know." Mrs Walsh bit her lip. This was the hard part. "I don't want to sound blunt, but frankly, Liz, Dan and I don't want to be responsible for April being suspended. I explained the situation to her tutor and she said that she'd really like to talk to the two of you to see if you can get to the bottom of it."

Mrs Gavin was cautious. "Talk to April's teacher about April?"

"Yes," Mrs Walsh said. "I've given her your number, she said she'll ring you either tomorrow or Wednesday. Fact is, if April doesn't apologise, you'll have to come here and sort it out yourselves. Dan and I can't be expected to . . ."

"Quite, quite," It was Mr Gavin back again. "I'm sure this is all nothing. April's a sensible girl, she's not stupid. Put her on and we'll sort this out right now."

Mrs Walsh was taken aback. "Well, eh, all right," she said. "I hope you'll have more success than I did. She wouldn't even talk . . ."

"Just get her," Mr Gavin sounded impatient.

"Please," he added.

Mary Walsh made a face. That man might be Dan's cousin but he was the bossiest person she'd ever come across. She put her hand over the receiver and called April.

When April appeared at the top of the stairs, she motioned to the phone. "Your dad," she said. "I phoned him to see if he could talk a bit of sense into you."

April's heart was pounding as she took the phone from Mrs Walsh.

"Hi, Dad?" She tried to keep her voice calm.

Her father wasted no time on niceties. "What's the story with the teacher?"

He didn't sound angry. But April said nothing, all the better to gauge his temper.

"Why on earth are you doing this, April?" he continued. "I can't believe you'd get suspended from a class, there must be a reason."

As he wasn't shouting at her, she attempted to

explain. "Mr Kavanagh, that's the teacher, he was being horrible to me and I just couldn't take it. Then . . . "

"He was being horrible?" Mr Gavin yelled. "You'd failed a test, for God's sake, how'd you expect him to be?"

April held the phone away from her ear. She made a face at the receiver and bit her lip to try and stop her tears. She knew he'd react like this. He wouldn't understand, he never listened to anyone, just thought that he knew . . .

"April, are you there?" Mr Gavin demanded.

"Uh-huh," April couldn't trust herself to speak.

"Uh-huh," her dad mimicked. "Go in and say sorry to that teacher tomorrow," he continued angrily. "If you don't, the Walshes want us to come over and sort this mess out. We'll have to go and talk to your tutor."

"That'll be a first," April muttered.

"What was that?"

"Nothing," April said hastily.

Her dad took a deep breath. "I really don't want to have to come over there, April," he continued. "I really don't." There was a second's silence before he added, "Do you understand me?"

April said nothing.

He took her silence as agreement, as she knew he would, and he said more calmly, "I'll ring tomorrow night to see how your apology went."

"But, Dad . . ."

"Bye, April. I'll ring tomorrow."

Luke came to a few minutes later. His ma and Davy must have half-carried, half-dragged him to the sofa – he didn't know how. Davy was staring at him from huge brown eyes.

"Where's Da?" Luke asked.

"Gone, gone for the night."

Luke tried to sit up but his head ached. "God, Ma, how did he find that bloody payslip? I usually burn 'em all."

"He found it in a pair of your Docs that you left in the kitchen. You must have forgotten to take it out."

Luke groaned. He remembered now. "You didn't tell him I gave you the money, did you?"

His ma shook her head and Luke nodded. "No point in the two of us gettin' to see the sunny side of his nature, is there?"

Mrs Coleman managed a smile. "I wish it had been me. I'm sorry, Luke." She held his hand against her face. Then she said, "He's taking all your money now – he said so."

"Damn," Luke bit his lip to stop the tears. He couldn't cry in front of his ma, she needed him.

Davy came over and touched Luke's face. "Poor Luke," he whispered.

"Yeah, poor flippin' Luke," he agreed bitterly.

Chapter Sixteen

The next evening, the call came. April had been dreading it all day.

"April, it's Dad."

"Hi." As if she wouldn't know who it was.

"Well, how'd it go?"

April played for time. "How'd what go?"

"The apology."

April felt weak. Even over the phone, she couldn't argue with him.

"You did apologise?" Her dad sounded impatient.

April gulped, "Eh, no. No, I didn't."

"Why?" he demanded. "I thought I told you to say sorry."

Very quietly but as firmly as she could, April said, "And I told you I couldn't."

"I hope this is a sick joke?"

April felt a tiny momentary thrill at annoying him. "It's not."

He hung up.

Five minutes later her mother rang.

"April," she breathed. "It's me. What on earth did you do to your father?" She lowered her voice. "He says you won't apologise to that teacher." She sounded almost tearful. "Why won't you apologise?"

April was reminded of the good cop, bad cop routine she saw in all the detective films.

"I can't say sorry to Mr Kavanagh, Mum," April replied flatly. "I just can't."

"But we'll have to come over now," her mother squealed. "Mary and Dan Walsh don't want the responsibility of having to deal with you. We'll have to get a flight booked, your father's work will suffer . . ." Her voice trailed off. She sighed. "I just don't understand."

It was always her dad's work! April could feel anger bubbling under the surface. It was no use, she'd tried to explain as much as she could but it was no use.

"April, are you still there?" her mother asked tentatively.

"Yes."

Her mother swallowed and hesitated before asking, "Are you sure things are all right?"

April felt stunned. This was the very question she had longed her to ask in Cork and she had never bothered. And now, now when things were great, when she actually had friends, her mother came out with it.

A few months too late, Mum, she thought.

"April?" she prompted.

"Things are fine," April replied. "I like Dublin a lot."

"Sure?" Mrs Gavin pressed gently.

April gulped. "There is one thing," she said, heart hammering. "There is something." It would be so easy to tell her mother. She wouldn't go off the deep end like her dad.

"Yes?" Her mother's voice was eager.

April felt as if her heart was about to burst. Her legs

grew shaky and her voice cracked. "It's about being a doctor."

"Yes?"

"Well . . ." April tried to find the words. She wondered would they have time for her at all if she let them down. "I . . ."

"Unless you get back into your biology class, you'll never make it," her mother said. "Your father would be so upset if you let your pride stand in the way of doing what you want."

It was always about them. Always. April couldn't listen any more.

"Bye, Mum," she said dully as she hung up.

She wondered if it would be so easy to dismiss them when they arrived over. The thought of it terrified her.

April called Luke for advice. The phone rang for a while before being picked up.

"Yeah?" The rough voice startled her.

"Is Luke in?" she asked. She figured that this man had to be Luke's father.

"Yeah, he's in. Do you want him?"

"Please."

The phone was put down and she could hear Mr Coleman yelling out Luke's name. It took a few seconds before Luke's voice came over the line. "Yeah?"

"Hi, Luke – it's April."

There was no answer.

"Luke?" she said again.

"Eh, April, this is not a good time, OK?" Luke sounded strange, distant.

"I just want to tell you about Dad. I need your help."

"Yeah, look, I'll ring, all right?"

"It won't take long," April felt a bit annoyed.

"Please, April, I can't talk. See you Friday?"

April said nothing. Friday was three days away.

"Friday?" Luke said again. "Please?"

"Forget it," April said as she put the phone down. She hoped he'd feel guilty.

Later that night, April went for a walk to clear her head. Her problems seemed to be piling up. She felt like laughing hysterically and crying at the same time. Her father had rung back and informed her that both he and her mother were coming over. They'd had a long talk with her tutor, agreed that something terrible had happened to her grades since her arrival in Dublin and now, like angels of mercy, they were flying in to assume control of her life again.

She felt so angry and so scared. The dreams were coming back too. Nightmares that she had left behind in Cork.

They hadn't sounded angry, her parents. Even her dad had calmed down. He actually sounded worried about her.

April didn't know how long she had walked for when, suddenly, just as she was about to cross the road, a huge motor-bike splashed into a puddle beside her. She was soaked and she shook her fist at the biker, who either did not see her or chose to ignore her. April began to scream every curse word she could think of at the biker and then, huge tears began to run down her cheeks. The more she tried to stop them, the more she cried.

On Friday Luke arrived at the Walshes to bring April out. He had a bunch of half-dead flowers that he had picked up during working hours. They had withered in the van. "A bit sad-lookin'," he said as he held them out to April. "A bit like me." He stopped and shrugged. "Sorry about the other day."

April led him into the front room where they could be on their own. She hadn't decided to be nice to him yet. "Why couldn't you talk?" she asked.

"Just stuff happened at home," Luke said casually.

"Like?"

Luke shrugged again. "Me da was in bad form, he was gettin' on me case."

"He sounded pretty mad on the phone, all right," April agreed. "What did you do?"

"Aw, answered him back or somethin'. I dunno. I forget."

Noticing a bruise on his arm, April asked, "How did you get that?" She pointed to the bruise. "It looks awful sore, what happened?"

Luke pulled the sleeve of his shirt down to cover it. "Something fell on me in work, hurt like hell."

April grinned. "Did Jimmy kiss it better?"

"Naw, I was savin' that job for you." Luke looked at her. "I really am sorry about Tuesday, I really am."

"Well, if you're half as sorry as these flowers look, I just might forgive you."

"Come here an' give us a kiss, so." Luke made to grab her and she darted away, laughing.

"Now's not a good time," she teased.

Chapter Seventeen

She was walking down a dark tunnel, damp floors and walls, narrow passageways. In front there was a spark of light and, as she got nearer, the light intensified. Running, panting, she reached out toward the light. Yelling, shouting, screaming that she was trapped. The passageway began to narrow – in order to pass, she had to turn sideways and walk. The roof of the tunnel was getting lower and lower so that she had to stoop, and still the light beckoned. Panic and sweat and terror and light, she knew she had taken the wrong turning . . .

April jerked awake, her heart hammering, the dream fragmenting as she tried to catch hold of it.

"You all right?" Sarah asked and April jumped.

"Fine. I'm fine, thanks," April shrugged. "I think I had a bad dream."

"You sure did," Sarah agreed. "You kept yellin' out. You were goin' on about lights an' stuff." She lowered her voice. "Don't let me da bother you. I know he's mad at you but it won't last." Then, yawning loudly, she stretched out her arms. She grimaced as the cold air hit her skin. "It's freezin' in here," she grumbled. "What's the time?"

"7.30," April replied. "Sorry for waking you."

112

"Naw, I was awake already. I'm nervous for the lads today; I hope they win."

It was the semi-final of the cup. Jack and the rest of the team had been training hard for the past week. Luke had turned up for most of the sessions, which surprised everyone. The lads had slagged him that it must be April's stabilising influence. "I think they've a good chance," April remarked. She had suddenly turned expert on the weaknesses and strengths of Ballinteer, which annoyed Sarah a bit.

"Is that 'cause Luke said so?" Sarah couldn't resist a joke.

"Mainly, yeah," April grinned at her. "He says the team they're playing are a bit crappy."

Sarah shrugged. Did April ever stop talking about Luke, she wondered? Was Luke as crazy about April as he let on? A gang of them had gone to the cinema in The Square last night, Luke and April included though, Sarah noted, April had paid for Luke. Still, she wondered if Frank stared after her the way Luke did with April. She figured glumly that the only way this would ever happen was if she stuck a picture of a Harley-Davidson on her backside. That would be sure to keep his attention.

April flung off her bedcovers. "I've a surprise for you," she announced as she delved behind her bed. She pulled up a huge blue-and-white banner and unfolded it. "I've the sticks for it under there, too," April indicated the bed.

Sarah was gobsmacked. "April, it's great! I love the lettering an' the drawings. It's brilliant!"

The words *Ballinteer United* were painted on the material in large black letters. April had also painted in caricatures of all the players. "I did it in art class,"

113

April explained. "We had to do a project and I did this. Luke gave me an old photo of the team to work from. Miss O'Reilly was thrilled with it. I spent all my lunch-times this week working on it."

"God, you can really paint," Sarah couldn't believe it. "The other team will have nothin' like this." Reverently she fingered the banner. Then she ran to the door as a thought struck her. "Have to tell Jack – I'll get him."

April laughed as Sarah bounded out the door and, without knocking, rushed into Jack's room and dragged him from his bed. April could hear him cursing and swearing at his sister as Sarah begged him to come into her room.

"Jack, stop that language this instant!" Mr Walsh had come in on the proceedings. He turned to his daughter. "Why on earth are you up so early?"

"Oh, Dad," Sarah beamed, "April has a great surprise for Jack – he has to come!"

"April is full of surprises, isn't she?" Mr Walsh muttered grumpily. To his daughter's annoyance, he continued, "And not particularly pleasant surprises, either."

Sarah laughed. "Morning grouch," she chided, trying to make him smile. "Anyhow," she tossed her head, "this is a nice surprise."

Dragging her father's arm, she propelled him to the bedroom. "DA–NA–NA–NAH!" she shouted.

April had put the flag against the wall. Mr Walsh gazed at it, rubbed his eyes and gazed again. "You did that?" he asked, sounding suitably impressed.

April blushed and nodded.

"JACK, JACK, GET IN HERE!" Mr Walsh yelled at the top of his voice, startling both girls. When Jack didn't reply, he went and dragged his son from the bed himself. Then he went and got his wife. All three crowded into the bedroom.

When Jack saw the banner he gave April a huge bear hug. "It's brilliant," he exclaimed as he and Sarah began to pick out who the various players were.

"I don't have a huge nose like tha'," Jack had spotted himself and was not impressed.

Sarah was giggling. "You do, it's a feckin' carrot should be stuck on your face and not a nose."

"I can think of somewhere better ta stick a carrot, up your . . . "

Jack was given a whack on the head from his mother. "You're getting worse, Jack," she hissed angrily.

"Might as well get up now an' get some brekkie." Jack ignored his mother.

"You making it?" she asked.

Jack laughed and said that he would.

April gazed at the four of them. None of her drawings had ever caused such excitement before. It was a strange feeling to have the four Walshes marvel at her work, but it was brilliant.

Even Mr Walsh was smiling, she noted with relief.

It was one of those crisp clear March days that seemed to herald the onset of spring. Sarah and April's breath puffed white as it carried into the calm air. Mr Walsh strode behind the two girls, smiling at their banter which he could hear. Frank was in step beside Mr Walsh but any effort at conversation was wasted on him. He hated football and he could not explain how Sarah had talked him into coming. Every so often Mr Walsh would glance in irritation at the lanky youth beside him. He was fervently hoping that no one would think he was his son.

115

When they reached the pitch, Sarah and April unfurled the banner. Some of the Ballinteer team were warming up on the pitch and they came over to see the banner that Jack had told them about. They began to search for their own faces on the flag.

"She flippin' makes Coleman the best-lookin' of us," Kev laughed. "That's favouritism for you."

"That's 'cause he *is* the best-looking," April said. She laughed as they roared, "UP YA GIRL YA" to her.

They called Luke over. He had just emerged from the dressing-room, and they began to make sloppy kissing noises. "She's bleedin' mad about you, Coleman," Stephen, one of the defenders, yelled.

"She's bleedin' mad, full stop," someone else piped up.

Luke grinned at April and nodded his head at the flag. "Great job."

"Thanks."

Luke's attention was drawn to Sarah. "How's it goin'?"

"Fine," Sarah as usual was monosyllabic.

Luke made a face at her that only April could see. She grinned back at him.

"I'd better head over to the rest of the lads," he said, as he touched April briefly on the arm. "I'll see you after the match, huh?"

"Sure." April watched him walk away. She had to admit, he was a fine thing, especially when his guard was down and his eyes smiled at her.

"Good luck today!" April called. Luke raised his hand in acknowledgement.

Mr Walsh gazed after the boy. There was something different about him that he couldn't put his

116

finger on. It was only later, when he pondered it over in his mind, that it came to him. The lad looked happy.

Despite Luke's prediction that Ballinteer would win, the match was a hard one.

There was no score after the first half. When the team came out in the second half, Luke had been put in a midfield-cum-striker position.

"He's there to get the ball and run down the pitch with it," Sarah explained to April. "He's at his best in midfield. I don't understand why Bill wouldn't let him play there in the first half."

April wouldn't have noticed that Luke was playing in a different position. Though she had gone to a few matches she still had a lot to learn. She really enjoyed the football, though, and her voice had become almost as loud as Sarah's.

"Hey, babe, keep the voice down, will ya?" Frank looked in astonishment at his girlfriend.

Sarah blushed and, nuzzling against him, explained that she couldn't help it.

April thought she would puke. Frank the Plank – Jack was right. Luke scored early in the second half. He lobbed the ball from halfway out on the pitch and caught the goalie off his line. The ball thumped on to the ground inside the net and the Ballinteer supporters went wild. Luke gave April the thumbs-up sign and she felt so proud of him. She could see what Sarah meant when she said that he was at his best in midfield. He was quick, agile and extremely skilful. No one could get a ball past him. His tackles were clean and deadly.

The second goal for Ballinteer came just before the end of the match. Luke got the ball, walked it right up the pitch and passed it inside for Jack, who powered it past the keeper. Ballinteer were into the final!

Jack and Kev came over and, grabbing the flag, proceeded to do a lap of honour, causing people to laugh and cheer. As Kev gave it back to April he said, "It brought us luck, bring it the next time."

April looked for Luke, but he was over talking to Bill and another man. She could see Luke shaking his head and Bill raising his hands in the air, as if in exasperation. The third man pressed something into Luke's hand and seemed to be appealing to him. Again, she could see Luke shake his head.

"For Christ's sake . . . " April heard Bill's voice carry on the wind, before the sentence was whipped away.

Luke threw the football down at Bill's feet and marched away from the two of them. His face was grim and he stalked into the dressing-room without looking in April's direction. Bill ran in after him. The other man shrugged, lit a cigar and walked away.

Half an hour later, Mr Walsh announced that he was going home. Luke had still not emerged and April said that she would wait for him.

"He's in awful form," Jack warned. "He had some kinda row with Bill."

"I'll wait."

"I think you'd better come with us," Mr Walsh said. "I don't like you waiting in the park on your own."

"I'll be fine – Luke will be out soon."

Mr Walsh glared at her. In his opinion, ever since she had started going out with Luke, there had been trouble.

118

All the same, he didn't want her to be around Luke in bad form. "We'll all hang on, so," he announced.

They waited another ten minutes. Reluctantly, Mr Walsh decided to leave. "You come straight back," he said. "If he's not out soon, give me a ring and I'll pick you up." He handed her his mobile.

"Thank you," April smiled at him. "Don't worry, I'll be fine." She watched them trudge toward the car park and then settled down to wait for Luke to show.

It took ten minutes. Bill emerged looking morose and Luke followed five minutes later. When he saw April, he closed his eyes and said, "Oh, shit, April, I forgot about you."

April bristled. "Thanks," she said shortly.

Luke walked over to her, swinging his sports bag but saying nothing.

"I think you could explain what kept you." April was annoyed. He hadn't even said "sorry" to her. "I've been waiting for the best part of an hour."

"I didn't ask you to bleedin' wait – did I?"

April was taken aback. "You did," she said. "You said, 'see you after the game', remember?"

Luke opened his arms wide. "Yeah, well, here I bleedin' am – you've seen me – satisfied?"

April didn't know whether to be hurt or angry. She looked at his irate face. "You – you fecker," she spat. "Don't you speak to me like that." When Luke made no response, she got really angry. "You are a right bastard!"

"Oooh, an obscenity," Luke jeered. "Have I driven you to that?"

April said nothing for a second. The hard mask of Luke's face did not change expression. "Forget it," she blurted out, nearly in tears. "Just forget it." She turned and stormed off.

Luke watched her leave.

"Don't bother coming around," April shouted, her back to him. "I know now what everyone means about you. It's over."

Luke watched her walk away. It was like he was watching a film, he could feel nothing at all. She grew smaller and smaller in the distance.

Then, with a stab of emotion, he knew that he couldn't let her go. He had never been as happy before in his life and here he was, treating the girl like dirt. He ran to catch up with her and heard himself yell, "God, April, I'm sorry. I really am."

April turned to face him. "So you should be. I waited an hour."

Luke shrugged. "I behaved like a thick, I'm sorry."

"You are a thick."

"Yeah." Luke held out his hand. There was a smile hovering about his lips. "Friends?"

"Don't ever treat me like that again." April was not budging.

"Sorry." Luke slowly lowered his hand.

Inwardly, April sighed. Thank you, God, she whispered. She would have died if he hadn't come after her. "What happened?" she asked.

"I don't want to talk about it."

"Fine," April's face fell and she took out the mobile phone. In a businesslike manner she began to dial the Walshes' number.

"What are you doin'?" Luke asked in amusement.

"I'm calling Mr Walsh, he told me he'd give me a lift home."

"I'll walk you home."

"No, thanks."

Luke looked stunned. He said sulkily, "I don't see wha' my rows have to do with you."

April shrugged. She knew she had the upper hand. "I only waited a flippin' hour. I get no apology, I was told to mind my own business, great!" She gave him what she hoped was a withering look and said wearily, "Get lost, Luke."

"I did apologise."

"Do you want a medal?"

Luke stared at her hopelessly. "I had a row with Bill."

"I'd never have guessed." April said, looking straight at him. "You are going out with me and you never, ever tell me things. I ask you the simplest questions about Davy and home and stuff and all I get is half-baked answers. You give me feck all! FECK ALL! Keep your secrets, then! Don't tell me what it was you had the row about. I only asked because I care."

Luke felt numb. She cared, he thought. Christ, that was a first. "He wants me to play professional." It was said quietly, but loud enough for her to hear.

"Huh?"

"He had a scout look at me."

"A scout?"

Luke turned his eyes upwards. "What is the point? You don't have a clue about football." Then, changing his mind, he added hastily, "A scout is someone who finds players. Each professional team has scouts. They come to a game an', if they like what they see, they ask you to come for a trial."

"And this guy wants you to try out for a real team?" April sounded impressed.

121

"Yeah, only Bill flips the lid when I say no."

"But why'd you say no?"

Luke clammed up. "You wanted to know what the row was about; well, that was it."

"Why did you say no?"

Luke sat down on a bench. To April's surprise, he put his head in his hands. "Stop, April," he groaned. "You're as bad as Bill." Then, looking at her, he said, "I said no 'cause I wanted to. I rowed with Bill 'cause he had bleedin' invited this scout to see me. He keeps tryin' to tempt me, he does me head in."

"How can he do your head in if you don't care about playing professionally?" April waited for him to reply and, when he didn't, went on, "You should be thrilled he thinks so much of you. What team was the scout from?"

"An English club." Luke knew April hadn't a clue, so he didn't elaborate further. "Don't tell anyone, please, April."

"Not if you don't want me to."

"Sorry for bein' so awful to you. I get like tha' sometimes. I'll never do it again, I promise."

April looked at him in exasperation. "I just can't figure why you won't make the best of yourself. If that was me, you wouldn't see me for dust. What do your parents think?"

"Dunno."

"You didn't tell them?"

Luke shook his head. "You may have noticed," he indicated the pitch, "they're not exactly football fans."

There was an awkward silence. Luke wouldn't look

at her. It was the first time he had ever volunteered information about his family.

"Do they never come to see you play?" April asked gently.

"Nope."

"But wouldn't your dad think it was great that you're Ballinteer's star player?"

"I doubt it'd make much impression on him," Luke said bitterly.

"Surely he'd be thrilled that you could play professionally – it's better than what you're doing now."

"Thanks," Luke said drily.

April took his hand. "I didn't mean it like that and you know it. I don't care what you do, but your dad must." She looked at him. "What about your mum, wouldn't she care?"

"I haven't told her. I'm not going to tell her. This conversation is a waste of time."

"Are you afraid to tell them or something?" April persisted.

"Just drop it, April," Luke said, trying to keep his voice level. "I don't see you rushing to tell your wonderful parents things either, so just drop it."

His remark stung. "Nice one."

Luke shrugged. "Yeah, well . . ."

"I wasn't being nosy – "

"Yeah, yeah, I know."

"I'm just puzzled. Your family seem a bit odd. I'm never invited to your house."

"You're missing nothing."

"I've never even met your mum."

Luke grinned. "When I propose I'll introduce you to the family, all righ'?"

April could feel her face redden. "That's not the reason . . ."

"It was a joke, April." Luke started to laugh. "I just love when you go all red," he slagged. "It suits you."

April smiled, his laugh was infectious.

As Luke looked at her, he felt his anger melt away. He wrapped his arms around her and held her tight against him. He never wanted to let go.

Chapter Eighteen

"Is April there, please, Sarah?" Mr Gavin's voice boomed with a heartiness he did not feel. April, his daughter, seemed to have vanished and night after night he found himself talking to a cold stranger on the other end of the line. There was something happening that he couldn't understand. He gave a start when he heard April utter a weary "Hi".

"It's me again," he announced. He lowered his voice. "I've the details of our travel arrangements here, I wonder if you want to take them down."

"OK." April found a pen. "Go ahead."

"Arriving into Dublin next Friday at six o'clock. Your mother and I'll go to our hotel, The Conrad, and we'll pick you up at eight pm for dinner there." He stopped and waited for her to say something. He kept hoping, each time he rang, that she'd tell him she would apologise. Then they could all forget this mess. But, as usual, April said nothing. He continued, "We can talk then, sort things out."

April gulped. Panic was setting in. They were coming. "I don't know what we'll say," she blurted. "I'm not saying 'sorry'."

Her dad ignored her outburst, though she heard an intake of breath on the other end of the line. "You'll stay in the hotel with us until this thing is sorted," he insisted.

April sighed. The cup-final was on the following day and she desperately wanted to go; however, she decided it wasn't the time to say so.

Mr Gavin waited again for a response and, getting none, he said, "Your mother wants a word."

April sighed. The same phone call every night. Her dad being bossy and her mother being sad and helpless.

"So, any crack?"

April smiled when she heard Luke's voice. She had thought it was her dad ringing, but thankfully it wasn't. "No," she answered. "Except that the CDs rang again."

They had christened April's parents the "Cork Dorks". Luke thought it was hilarious the way they rang her every night. "The amount they're payin' on phone bills, they could have flown home ten times over by now," he slagged. "What did they say this time?"

"Guess."

"Apologise now or else?"

"Got it in one." April sighed. "I'm worried about them coming, Luke. I know my dad'll go mental. My mum'll have a fit when she sees my clothes." April had spent most of her pocket money on new clothes. "I feel sick every time I think of it."

"Stick to your guns, April," Luke advised. "You've come this far, don't let them get to you. Anyhow, they can't be that bad." He stopped for a second, then continued solemnly, "They must love you, anyhow, they seem awful worried."

April nearly laughed. "Sure."

"I'm serious," Luke said. "They care about you."

"Well," April said shortly, "I wish they didn't, it'd make life a lot easier."

Her comment upset Luke but he didn't want to row with her – that was the last thing she needed. He just said, "Maybe, maybe not." Then, without waiting for her to reply, he said, "Listen, have to go. See you tomorrow?"

"Yeah, see you," April replied, wondering what on earth she had said to make him rush off like that.

The phone rang.

"If that's the CDs, I'm not here," April whispered to Sarah. "I can't talk to them again. Dad was in foul humour yesterday."

"Right," Sarah giggled and went to answer the phone.

"Hello, Sarah," Mr Gavin said. "Is April there?"

"Eh, no." Sarah tried not to laugh. The phone calls were becoming a bit of a joke; even her dad had said that the phone could nearly connect up with Germany by itself at eight every evening.

"When will she be back?"

Sarah gulped. "Eh, late. Very late."

Mr Gavin was suspicious. "Where is she? What's she doing out late on a school night?"

"She is doing . . . some . . . eh . . . schoolwork," Sarah faltered. Then, on a triumphant note, she added, "Study, she's studying."

"Oh," Mr Gavin was at a loss. "Great, that's good to hear. In a study group?"

"Yes. Yes, a group." Sarah wanted to get off the phone in case he'd think of other awkward questions.

"I just want to check that she knows it's this Friday we're arriving," Mr Gavin said.

"Oh, she knows," Sarah said. "She keeps talking about it."

"Good," Mr Gavin sounded pleased. "Tell her we rang, won't you?"

"The second I see her," Sarah promised in a sweet voice. "Bye now. See you Friday."

"Looking forward to it," Mr Gavin said.

"Your da's so sweet," Sarah said to April as she put down the phone.

"Yeah, the way a lion looks sweet," April said glumly.

Chapter Nineteen

April arrived home from school and flung her bag across the bed. She felt sicker than she had ever felt in her life. Her mother and father were arriving that night. They had been on the phone to her every evening, asking her questions about school, about study. They ranted, they shouted, they pleaded. April remained resolute: the only feeling she had was anger. She couldn't believe how angry she felt listening to them.

They were going to sort it all out. Her stomach had been churning from the moment she had got up that morning.

They were bringing her out for dinner.

They would discuss things after dinner.

They were arriving in less than four hours. They said they really wanted to see her.

April said she couldn't wait to see them.

Oh, God, she was going to puke.

Opening her wardrobe, April tearfully looked at her "pre-new-found-popularity" clothes, as she jokingly termed them. How she hated all those things her mother had bought her.

She absently fingered a blouse that was about a size too small and suddenly she felt so tired. What, she wondered, was the point of the past few weeks? Her mother and father were coming to wash her away. Coming to clean up the "mess" she'd made.

Jimmy dropped Luke off at The Coach House. "I'm gettin' out here," Jimmy explained. "I need to grab a sambo for me tea."

Luke tried not to laugh. Jimmy was living on sandwiches these days. His wife had left him last weekend, taking their "sixteen-year-old brat" with her. "I'll only take her back on condition that she leaves him behind," Jimmy had chortled, the first week he was left to his own devices. Luke had a feeling that Jimmy would roll out the red carpet if his wife even offered to cook for him at this stage.

"Maybe this might be your lucky weekend, Jim," Luke grinned as he prepared to walk home. "Maybe she'll realise what a catch you really were all these years."

Jimmy shrugged. "I wouldn't bleedin' mind if she only told me why she left," he replied.

"Women, you'd never understand them." Luke tried to sound consoling. He watched Jimmy enter the pub and then, shoving his hands into the pockets of his tattered jeans, he slowly began to walk home.

Luke thought how ironic his last parting words to Jimmy were. April totally baffled him. She was like a jigsaw with a piece missing. Just when he thought he'd got the picture, a chunk of it didn't make sense. He couldn't understand why she wouldn't tell her folks what she really wanted; he couldn't make out why, if she didn't want her folks coming over, she wouldn't just say sorry to Kavanagh. But he didn't like rowing with her, so he'd kept his mouth shut and told her she was great.

Which she was.

She had changed since their first meeting, he thought. He liked her even better now. She was madder, funnier and, he searched for the word . . . happier. He hoped it was because of him.

Of course, Luke knew that she had changed him as well. He was less angry, a lot funnier, the person he might have been if he hadn't to go home every evening.

Luke sighed. April's parents were arriving that night; the day before the cup final, for Christ's sake! He hoped she'd be able to make it to the match. Bill had warned the team to stay in, not to drink, and told them all jokingly to stay away from women.

Luke decided to call over to April that evening, as a surprise, just to wish her luck. She needed a surprise, she was very down last night. Another bleedin' nice thought, he grinned to himself.

The smile disappeared from his face as he neared home. His da was tinkering about with his car. Luke tried to get by without talking but his ould fella was in a sociable mood. He held up a new car stereo. "Guess how I got this?" he sneered.

Luke wondered how much rudeness he could get away with. He decided not a lot, if he wanted to see April this evening. "Dunno."

"Cost about," his da screwed his face up, "about one hundred and ten quid."

Luke shrugged again, his heart twisting. He turned away and went inside to the sound of his da laughing to himself.

April sat on the bed. Her stomach seemed to have taken up aerobics, it was churning about so much. She jumped when the door banged open.

"Only me," Sarah said breezily. She stood gawking at April. "You look cool, those hipsters are really nice on you." She told April to stand up. She walked all around her. "I think you lost weight," she declared. "You look as skinny as anything in them."

"Yeah, I lost about six pounds," April confirmed. "I've been so worried about tonight. It's the nicest thing the CDs have done for me in ages – made me look skinny."

They both laughed. In the silence that followed, Sarah threw her arms impulsively around April. "Good luck," she said as she hugged her. "You were right to do what you did."

"Thanks," April said, touched. "I wish you were coming with me to back me up."

"You'll be fine," Sarah said. "They'll understand."

"I dunno . . . " April said bleakly.

There was something about April that seemed different tonight, Sarah thought, but she couldn't identify what it was. She put her hand on April's shoulder, saying, "It won't be that bad."

They both jumped as the doorbell rang. Sarah ran to the window. "There's a car outside, I think it's them," she said breathlessly. "Yeah, a woman and a man are getting out, but, hang on, they're going in next door. Naw, they don't even look like your folks."

April began to breathe again.

Mrs Walsh yelled up the stairs. "April, Luke is here."

"Oh, God, what on earth is he doing here!" April said, panicking. "God, he's going to run straight into Mum and Dad."

"April!" Mrs Walsh yelled again.

"Coming!"

She made her way downstairs. Luke was standing in

the hall. He grinned at her. "You look gorgeous," he smiled.

"What are you doing here? They're coming any second now," April hissed. "God, Luke, they'll kill me if they think I'm going out with someone. No, hang on, they'll probably kill you."

Luke looked hurt. "Only came to wish you luck," he said, offended.

"Oh, Luke, I'm sorry," April gave him a quick hug. "It's really nice of you to come over. Thanks." She paused. "It's just with them coming, I'm in bits. Sorry for snapping at you."

She looked at his sullen face. Luke hurt easily. "Sorry," she said again, softly.

"Forget it," Luke cracked a grin. "I like when gorgeous girls snap at me."

Mrs Walsh arrived into the hall. "Will you bring the lad into the front room," she said to April. "He'll freeze out here."

"I was just leavin'," Luke said. He was never comfortable in this house. He knew what they thought of him.

The bell rang and both April and Luke jumped.

"Well, open the door," Mrs Walsh ordered. Neither of them moved so, edging past them, she answered the door herself.

April heard the rumble of her father's voice. Mrs Walsh laughed at something he said and then ushered April's parents into the hall. "Come in, come in," she exclaimed. "It's great to see you."

"Likewise," Mr Gavin agreed as he entered the house. Mr Walsh and Jack came out of the TV room to say hello and Sarah appeared at the top of the stairs.

April could feel her heart pounding as she saw her

father examine her. "April," he acknowledged, nodding at her formally.

He looked grim, she thought, her heart sinking. She nodded back. He gave her an awkward hug.

"How are you, darling?" Mrs Gavin gushed. After kissing April on both cheeks, she looked her up and down. Her eyes grew wide when she saw what April was wearing. "Where on earth did you get those trousers?" she exclaimed. Turning to Mrs Walsh, she rolled her eyes dramatically as she said, "Honestly, teenagers."

"I think they look great on her," Sarah said loyally. "They really suit her."

April smiled at her gratefully.

Mrs Gavin said nothing, her mouth a thin line of disapproval.

"Eh, gotta go," Luke tried tactfully to reach the door without being noticed.

Mrs Walsh turned to the Gavins. "Sorry," she apologised. "I never introduced Luke to you. Luke, these are April's parents. Jim, Liz, meet Luke."

Luke nodded. "How's it goin'?" He made another attempt to escape.

"Friend of Jack's, are you?" Mr Gavin asked pleasantly.

"Eh, yeah," Luke nodded.

"More a friend of April's, I think," Dan Walsh said pointedly.

"Pardon?" Mr Gavin said, startled.

"Luke is April's boyfriend," Mr Walsh said, emphasising each word. "He has been since she came here."

"Da!" Sarah exclaimed. "God!"

134

"He's my friend, too," Jack announced, feeling sorry for April. "He came over to see me tonight."

"Really," Mr Gavin said dryly. He was shocked. To think his daughter would go for a lad like that. And how come he'd never been told of him?

Luke was glaring at him sullenly. He felt trapped.

Suddenly, a light seemed to go off inside Mr Gavin's head. The pieces all began to fit into place. I've been so blind, Jim Gavin thought. It had to be this Luke fella that was leading April astray. Impulsively and in his nicest voice, he said, "Perhaps Luke would like to join us tonight?"

Luke stared at him in disbelief. "No, no, thanks," he mumbled. "I was just headin' off."

"Oh, come on," he cajoled, "It's only dinner." He looked at Luke's jeans and sweatshirt. "What you're wearing will be fine," he said, sounding totally unconvincing.

"He was goin' out with me tonight," Jack announced suddenly and Luke grinned gratefully.

"I'm sure you'll be able to give it a miss."

Jack glowered at April's dad. "I was goin' to," he replied. "Both of us are playin' a big match tomorrow an' we have to rest, don't we, Coleman?"

"Yep."

"It'll be a quiet night," Mr Gavin smiled. "Besides, I'm sure April would like Luke along." He looked at his daughter.

April gulped. She had forgotten how forceful her dad was. "I don't think . . . " she began but he waved her answer away with his hand.

"Don't want your own boyfriend there?" he chortled, as if this was a great joke. "Well, some relationship that is."

Luke glanced desperately at April.

135

"Well?" Mr Gavin asked again.

Luke shrugged. It would look rude if he refused and he didn't want them to get mad at April because of him.

"Yeah, sure," he muttered. Then, in a fit of bravado he took April's hand. He saw the looks pass between her parents and it pleased him. He gave April's hand a gentle squeeze but she didn't squeeze his back.

April sat in the back seat of the rented car, Luke at her side.

She couldn't bear to look at him.

"So, Luke," April jumped at her dad's voice, "what exactly do you do? Are you still in school? Do you work?" He fired the questions at a startled Luke. "I mean, no one told us about you."

"He's in the meat trade," April answered quickly.

"The meat trade," Mr Gavin nodded, his eyes still fixed on the road. "What do you do, anything interesting?"

"Transport," April jumped in again.

Luke give her a puzzled look, wondering why she wouldn't let him answer for himself, but he said nothing.

April continued, still not looking in Luke's direction. "He's involved in the transport and general sale of meat in the western area of the country." That sounded good, her dad was bound to be impressed.

He was. "The whole western area, you're responsible?"

"Sounds important," Mrs Gavin interjected.

Luke shrugged.

"Modesty," April said, nudging him.

To her horror, Luke moved away and began to stare out the car window. April bit her lip, she could see his

136

hands all balled up, his face set in a hard mask. This was going to be some evening . . .

Luke had to bite his bottom lip hard to stop from yelling out. April wouldn't let him get a word in edgeways. Her da had jokingly told her to let "the lad" answer for himself. Some bleedin' chance! According to April, he was a business tycoon, a meat magician, and well on his way to earning his first million. Luke wondered why she was telling all these lies – was she ashamed of him or something? She would hardly even look at him. Luke felt like getting out of the car there and then, but it was too late.

"Here we are," Mr Gavin announced as he pulled up outside the hotel, parked the car and ushered everyone in front of him. Luke could feel Mr G's eyes on him again – probably wondering why I can't afford better stuff to wear on the huge salary I'm makin', he thought.

Conversation stopped as they waited to be seated.

It wasn't a nice easy silence, it was a silence in which unsaid things seemed to be growing more powerful as time went on. Luke could see Mr and Mrs G gazing at April, their faces betraying their anxiety. He felt almost sorry for them.

A smiling waitress arrived and showed them where to sit. She handed them their menus. Luke decided to get whatever the others were having – he felt out of his depth in all this grandeur. He looked totally out of place in the gear he was wearing, probably exactly the way Mr Gavin wanted it. Luke just wanted to be sitting in Supermac's, with a burger in his hands and a Coke on the table. There was no fear of gettin' a burger in this joint, he thought glumly.

April forced every morsel of food down her throat in order not to appear nervous. She knew what was coming – her father was dying to get on to the main issue of the visit, namely her studies. He was chomping at the bit. It was the worst meal she had ever sat through. Luke had remained silent throughout, barely eating his dinner. In normal circumstances, April would have slagged him about it. Luke liked plain food, here there was sauce on everything. Luke was deeply suspicious of sauces.

April felt her stomach heave as her father sat back in his chair, sipped on a glass of red wine and said casually, "I think we should really talk now, April. We can hardly go through the whole weekend avoiding the issue, can we?"

April gulped. She tried to appear calm, she couldn't bear Luke to sense her fear. "I don't think it's fair on Luke," April whispered, her voice cracking. She wanted her dad to see that she was willing, more than willing to discuss the subject, but that Luke would be embarrassed by it all.

Mr Gavin shook his head. He turned his gaze on Luke. It was cold and hard. "On the contrary, I think Luke should be here. Maybe he knows something we don't?" He raised his eyebrows questioningly. When Luke didn't answer, he turned impatiently away from him. "So," he lit his cigar, "what is all this nonsense about?" He blew smoke into the air.

"Nonsense?" April played for time. "I don't . . ."

"With the teacher," Mr Gavin barked. "What do you mean by cheeking a teacher?"

Luke felt his hands curl into fists. "Now, hang on . . ." he tried to intervene.

Mrs Gavin gave him a disdainful look. "Let April answer," she ordered.

Luke turned to April. Her head was bent and he couldn't see her face. "Tell them," he urged. "Tell them about how he was unfair to you."

"Unfair?" Mr Gavin laughed. "The man was probably only doing his job." He leaned across the table to April. "You will apologise to that man first thing on Monday – is that understood?" April stared at the table.

"All right?" Mr Gavin's voice was rising.

"Dad? If you'll just let . . . "

"ALL RIGHT?"

Diners at other tables stared curiously in their direction. Mr Gavin ignored them. "You will apologise," he ordered, his voice low but forceful.

Luke saw April nod. He had to blink to be sure he had seen her agree to something that she had sworn she would never do. He felt like shaking her. What was the point of her parents coming all this way? She could have said sorry weeks ago and saved them all the hassle. "April?" he asked uncertainly. She ignored him. He turned to her parents. "Don't you even care why she did what she did?" he asked.

Mr Gavin turned to him. Luke flinched at the open contempt on his face. He pointed his finger in Luke's direction. "I care when my daughter starts ruining her chances in school, that's what I care about." He took April's hand in his. His voice softened. "She's wanted to be a doctor since she was six, do you know that?"

Luke shook his head.

"She is clever." He turned to April. "You are, you know you are." There was silence. Mr Gavin was baffled. "I certainly hope that you're not keeping April away from her books," he said to Luke. "I mean it's

139

only since she came here . . . " He let the implication hang in the air.

Luke refused to be baited.

Mr Gavin tried a more reasonable approach. "You've a good job, you must realise how important an education is?"

Luke looked desperately at April. He didn't know whether to lie and say "yes, he did know the value of education" and land April in it, or say "no" and end the whole bloody charade. "Well, if she's not up to the work, why force her?"

He knew he had said the wrong thing when Mrs Gavin turned around and retorted, "Who's forcing her? What do you mean by that? Are you saying that we're forcing her to do anything?"

Luke wanted to laugh. He knew how to put his two feet in it, right enough.

Mrs Gavin turned to April. "Do you feel we're forcing you into anything?"

April said nothing. Mrs Gavin turned triumphantly to Luke. "There you are," she declared, "We're not forcing her to do anything, we're only trying to understand why she's suddenly not doing too well in school." She looked pointedly at Luke.

Luke shrugged. "I don't know much about education, actually," he answered. "I left after me Junior." If April wanted to lie, fine. If she was ashamed of him, fine. But he wasn't putting on an act for these two snobby eejits.

There was a horrified silence.

Mr Gavin stared hard at him. "Well, you must be a bright lad to land on your feet in a good job, so."

"It's a lousy job an' I didn't leave school, I was expelled for joyridin'."

April's head shot up. Her eyes glistened with unshed

140

tears and something else Luke couldn't place. He didn't know what she was feeling. Turning defiantly toward her parents, Luke saw that they literally had their mouths wide open.

Mr Gavin appeared to be smiling slightly. "So that's the reason," he pronounced grandly. "I knew it. You're turning my daughter against school, aren't you?"

"Naw."

"Oh, really?" Mr Gavin's voice dripped with sarcasm, "You explain to me then how my straight 'A' daughter suddenly starts getting 'B's'."

Luke shrugged. "I dunno," he answered.

Mr Gavin turned to April. "Nice company you're keeping," he said sarcastically.

April looked at them, her face white. "I . . . I . . . I didn't know . . . "

"Know what?" her mother asked.

"Know about him." April nodded at Luke. She wouldn't look at him.

Luke gasped. He felt as if he had been hit. "You did," he muttered in disbelief.

"Has he been putting you off your work?" Mr Gavin's voice was gentle. He looked sympathetically at his daughter.

Luke waited.

A barely perceptible nod of the head.

"Liar," he spat out, startling them all. April looked at him and suddenly Luke understood. How could he have been so blind? The girl was petrified. He should have known; he, better than anyone, knew how it felt. Lead feet, afraid to move. Still, he couldn't let her ruin her life over them. He wasn't afraid of them, he could speak up. He felt anger burning deep inside, anger at these two people, anger at his own ma, anger at his da and, most of

141

all, anger at the mess his own life was in. "She's lyin'." Luke forced April's head up with his hand and continued, "You know nothin' about her. You know nothin' about April." He stopped and looked at April. "That girl is not the girl I know."

April wrenched her head away from him and began to knead the tablecloth with her fingers.

"The April I know wants to do art for a start, not medicine." Luke savoured the shock on their faces. "She won't tell you, though – I guess she's afraid – an' who would blame her, huh?" He stared at Mr Gavin. "April told me she can't tell you anythin', an' after tonight I'm not surprised. You're a bossy bastard, do you know tha'?" Catching April's eye, he continued, "There, I said it for you, April. Don't mess up your life; I said it for you."

Luke stood up to leave. He couldn't stand scenes. He had to get away, he felt so angry. He hadn't been this angry since he got expelled. He glanced at the Gavins. They looked mortified. Everyone in the restaurant was gawking and the manager was on his way over. "They know now, April," Luke said before he stormed out, nearly knocking the manager over on his way.

Chapter Twenty

There was silence when Luke left. April became conscious of her heartbeat and, far away, the muffled voices of other diners. She felt drained and sick, afraid to look up, afraid to talk.

"What on earth was that fella on about?" Mr Gavin asked in a bemused voice. "God almighty, April, what on earth was he saying?"

April took out a tissue and began wiping a lone tear that had slipped out of the corner of her eye. They still didn't get it. They would rather blame Luke for his outburst than face the facts. April knew it was now or never. She wished Luke was there, but he wasn't. She had lied to him shamelessly, terrified that he would reject her if he saw she was afraid, pretending to be concerned about her parent's feelings when, all the time, fear ate her up. She had to stand up to them, face to face.

"Well?" her father demanded. "That lad is nothing but a hooligan. Expelled from school!" He glared at April. "What are you doing, going around with the likes of that?"

"Yes," Mrs Gavin said. "My God, April, I thought we brought you up better than that."

April felt angry. An anger that until that moment she

had never known she harboured. Her head shot up and she glowered at her parents. "Brought me up?" she said, in a voice so low it was almost inaudible. "Brought me up? You never brought me up. You were never there for me, EVER. Your friends brought me up so don't take credit for me."

"April . . . ?"

"Luke was right. I don't want to do medicine." She stood up from the table and shied away as her mother reached for her. "Don't," she whispered, "just don't touch me."

With that April threw her napkin on the table and stood up to leave. "I'm going to find Luke," she announced, "the hooligan." She turned to her dad. "Now you know, Dad. You've got the answers you came for, I hope you're happy."

Luke caught a 48A and sat morosely in the back seat. He should have known how frightened April was; he kicked himself for not guessing.

Luke felt so fed up and angry. He felt like doing something, something bad . . . he always did mad things when he got really angry. The last time was when his da had shoved his ma through a glass door in the house. Luke had tried to stop him, but his da was a big man. His ma ended up in hospital and he had been beaten every night of her stay there. Soon after, he had taken the teacher's car and very nearly succeeded in killing himself . . . then his da had broken his arm for him last November. Luke had to tell everybody that he had broken it in work.

His da kept saying that if he, Luke, left home, he would beat his wife and Davy all the time. "Don't think just 'cause yer on wages now that you can desert me," he had threatened.

Luke was trapped. He wouldn't leave his ma and Davy, anyhow. If he could keep the three of them in a flat on his wages he would have, but a hundred and ten quid, plus any money his ma might get, was not enough.

Luke wondered why his ma just didn't do a runner, but he never asked her. She could have gone into a shelter, but his ma had her pride. She never let on that anything was wrong and she expected her kids to do likewise.

April ran out into the cool night air. She didn't care that it was late at night and that Dublin could be a dangerous place when it got dark. She didn't care about anything except finding Luke and apologising to him for the way she had practically disowned him in front of her parents. Talk about the Judas-kiss!

She was vaguely aware of voices behind her as she bolted down Grafton Street toward the 48A bus stop.

Her father caught her first. She struggled to escape from his arms, but he held her tight. "Please, April," he gasped. "Please don't run out on us – don't do this."

His voice sounded as if he would cry.

April looked at him, puzzled, and he let her go. April thought that he didn't look like her dad, he just looked like a sad old man. "We're not good at talking in our family, are we?" he asked sadly.

April shook her head.

"I often wanted to tell you things, you know, things like how much we, eh, missed you, when we were away." He gazed down at his shoes. "I couldn't, so I talked about your study instead. It's all I ever talk about to you, I just can't help it."

April said nothing.

"Your mother has cried nearly every night since we left, do you know that?"

"No," April whispered.

"It's true," Mrs Gavin nodded in agreement. Her eyes were sparkly with tears. She had arrived just in time to hear her husband's remark and she stood, high-heeled shoes in her hands, unsure of what to do.

"Neither of us are particularly good with children," Mr Gavin continued. "When you arrived, well, we were a bit shocked. We loved you, but we just couldn't seem to manage you." He scratched his head. "I know I'm away a lot, but we do keep in touch. We feel we know what you're at."

April felt like laughing. She wished she could laugh and laugh and never stop. They knew what she was at? They hadn't a clue!

"I love my work and when you showed an interest . . ."

"At six years old," April interrupted him.

"Yes, at six; well, I thought, good, common ground. I can chat to my daughter about this. Your mother did the same. She thought you liked shopping for clothes and so she brought you along . . ." He stopped. "It was easier that way, I suppose. We didn't, don't, know how to handle you."

It was hard for him to admit. April could feel his hurt and she felt sorry for him. But she wanted to hit him, she wanted to hurt him. They had let her down so badly.

She was about to say so when her mother blurted out, "It's not that we don't love you – we do, we love you a lot."

It was in that instant April knew that, in some strange way, her parents did care.

Maybe she could tell them things.

Maybe she would take a chance.

"Where are his keys?"

The telephone began to ring and they both ignored it.

"What are you doin' home so early?" Mrs Coleman asked. "I thought you were goin' inta town or somethin'."

"I want his keys."

"What keys?" Mrs Coleman stalled for time. Luke looked strange. She hated when he was in one of these moods – it always spelled trouble.

"How many bloody keys does he have?" Luke snarled. "I want his feckin' car keys." He began to look under all the stuff piled up on the mantelpiece. Some papers floated to the ground and he ignored them. Then he strode into the kitchen and opened all the drawers, scattering everything.

"What do you want them for?" Mrs Coleman asked, following him. "Please, Luke, don't do anything foolish."

The telephone stopped ringing and started up again seconds later. He ignored her and went on searching.

Eventually, he found them on top of the fridge. "See you, Ma, I'm goin' for a little spin around." He gave her a twisted grin and made for the door.

She blocked his way. "Oh, dear God, Luke, please," she begged. "What's happened? Oh, God, don't, please."

Luke stared at her. "I'm goin'. I have to go – you can come if you want."

"Luke, are you mad?" she whispered. "He'll kill you." Her voice took on a hysterical note as she grabbed his arm. "Luke, don't."

"Comin'?"

She knew she was beaten. Her shoulders slumped and her head dropped.

"Come on, Ma," Luke urged. He was grinning now. "How many times have you ever been in that car? Anyhow, by right it's mine, he pays for it outa my money, you know."

Mrs Coleman didn't want to go with him, but she was afraid not to – what if he did something mad, like the last time . . . at least she could try and stop him. "I'll get Davy," she muttered.

"The more the merrier," Luke laughed.

Mrs Coleman gazed at her son and wondered what he was planning.

They walked back to the hotel in silence, Mr and Mrs Gavin on either side of their daughter. They were afraid to touch her in case she ran away again. They just wanted her to stay with them.

The manager of the restaurant was not pleased when they arrived in again. He said tactfully that he hoped there would be no more trouble, before handing the bill to April's father.

"Put it on my tab," Mr Gavin said airily, as he made his way towards the lift to bring them to their room.

In the room, he poured the three of them some coffee and they sipped it quietly. No one wanted to break the silence.

"So," Mr Gavin eventually said, as he clasped both his hands together. "Are you going to talk?" he looked intently at April.

"I . . . I don't know where to start . . . " she faltered. The idea of talking to them unnerved her. The things she wanted to talk about made her tremble – the memories, the hurt, the rejection.

"Start anywhere," her father said, in what was for him a gentle tone. "Start with what that lad said, what was his name? Duke?"

They couldn't even be bothered to remember.

"Luke," her mother spoke up. "It was Luke."

"OK, Luke," her dad said. "Start with what he said."

April had never in her life been asked to explain anything to her parents. The prospect daunted her. She began to twirl a strand of hair around her finger. "I don't want to do medicine," she said haltingly. She took a deeper breath and said more forcefully, "I just never really wanted to do it." The feelings that coursed through her took her breath away. It was like flying, it was like being dizzy. She said a third time, "I thought I wanted it once, but not now."

Silence.

April screwed up the courage to look at her parents; she saw that her dad looked hurt, her mother sad. She knew what would happen, they'd be so disappointed they wouldn't be interested in her any more.

"Why didn't you ever tell us?" her dad said, shell-shocked. "Were we so terrible that you couldn't say?"

April felt as if time slowed down. Her senses heightened. She looked both of them in the eye and asked, "Do you know what one of the happiest days of my life was?"

When they didn't answer, she continued in a subdued voice. "It was when I was six years old and you," she turned to her dad, "you brought me into your work. You showed me your office and the hospital where you worked and you talked to me." She stopped. "You talked to me and I felt so important. For the first time in my life, I felt you liked me. On the way home, I told you that I wanted to be a doctor and your whole face lit up. I felt I had done something right. Something good. Something to make you want to stay at home with me." April's voice broke. "Then, as I grew older, I knew that all I had to do was mention your work and you'd talk to me. I wanted to make you both proud of me 'cause, well . . . " April couldn't continue. It hurt too much to say.

"Because you thought we didn't care?" It was her mother.

"Yeah," April muttered. "Always all over the world, me left at home with anyone who'd take me."

"That's not true," Mr Gavin defended himself. "They were all good friends."

"You badgered everyone to take me in – I could hear you on the phone day and night. It was embarrassing, I hated going to those people." April began to rub her hands together. "Then, when your welcome ran out in Cork, I'm dumped in Dublin." April worked up enough courage to glare at her dad. "You hardly ever saw Mr Walsh and yet you bossed his family into taking me, just like you boss everyone. Like you boss me."

Mr Gavin couldn't reply. What she was saying was true, only he'd never looked at it like that before.

"It still doesn't explain why you're in so much trouble up here," her mother said. "Why did you cheek the teacher like that?"

"Because he was bullying me, bossing me," the words tore out of her mouth. April began to shake. "No one is ever going to bully me again, no one."

"Now, hang on a minute." Her father stood up. "If you're suggesting that I bullied you . . . "

"NO, AT SCHOOL, EVERYONE . . . " April began to cry, loud wrenching sobs. She felt her mother's arms going around her and her crying grew louder. Her mother held her for a long time until April began to calm down.

"At school, what?" her father asked.

Wiping her eyes with a shaky hand, April began to speak. Slowly at first, like she was stepping on ice, then as the ice held firm, she began to talk faster and faster, spilling it all out. Wanting them to know, wanting them to be shocked, wanting them to tell her it was going to be all right. "It was OK at first," she said, "first year was all right. Then one of the lads said, for a joke, he was going to open a book on where I would be staying the next time you both took off."

"What?"

April ignored the outburst. "It started out as a joke, then they really did start taking bets. Then one of the girls, Mary, she began to ask me if I had homework and stuff done – she wanted to borrow it. So I let her have it. Everyday after that she'd ask for it, so one day I told her 'No', that she'd have to do her own homework." April paused and blinked rapidly before continuing, "She met me after school that day, robbed my bag and threw all my books into the stream by the school. I spent ages trying to dry them and the next day, before school, she took all my homework and poured ink over it. She had a load of girls with her, I couldn't fight back. From then on, I just gave in."

"And you never told us?"

Again April continued as if she didn't hear. "Whatever Mary said everyone did – they were all afraid, I guess. She began to call me names, like 'Pass the parcel' and stuff like that. She laughed at my clothes and my hair, just about everything I had. The others let her; it wasn't cool to be on my side, I was the nerd, the swot." She gazed at her dad. "I got great results in my work 'cause I had no friends, no one to go out with, no one to have a laugh with. I just stayed in and studied, it kinda made me forget what my life was like." April took a deep breath. "Last year," she said, "things got really bad. Mary and her pals would follow me home from school and push me about or throw stuff at me. It wasn't that they hurt me, it was just that I was so scared all the time. I was afraid to walk down the road in case I'd meet them.

"Then," her voice faltered, "one day, John Byrne asks me out. I couldn't believe it, the most popular guy in class asks me out. Like an eejit I said 'yeah'." April bit her lip. "He never turned up. I waited where he told me to, but he never turned up. It was a joke, just a joke." April could feel the hurt all over again. "After that, I didn't care what they did to me. Then you and Mum arrived back, full of chat and presents and I just felt so broken. You never asked me how I was or anything."

April stopped. It was all out. She felt as if she'd shrunk somehow, the tension was gone.

"Why didn't you give us a hint?" her father asked, bewildered. "My God, April, we've really, really failed you." He put his head in his hands and his body began to shake. "My lovely girl," he whispered. "How could they . . ."

April's heart went out to him. Her parents had only done what they thought best. They did love her, she knew it now. Reaching out, she stroked his sleeve. "It's OK, Dad," she said softly. "I'm OK now, sort of. I came here and no one knew me. They let me be myself. I didn't have to watch my back all the time, people actually liked me. The Walshes cared," she faltered, "And Luke cared. He stood up for me tonight." Her eyes filled with tears.

"And what do you want to do?" Mrs Gavin asked, stroking her daughter's hair. "With your life, April, what do you want to do?"

April swallowed. This was the moment of truth. She gathered her courage and said quietly, "Paint. I want to paint."

Mr Gavin stared at her. "Paint?" he said faintly. "You want to paint *pictures*?" He tried to be reasonable. "Artists live in poverty."

April would have laughed if it wasn't such a serious issue. "I just can't go living a lie any more, Dad," she said nervously. "I'd never make a doctor, I get sick just looking at *ER*."

There was silence. April thought it would never end. She knew they were disappointed at her and she wondered if they'd have time for her at all now?

Glancing up quickly, she saw that her dad was standing with his back to them, his hands in his pockets of his suit, his head down. Her mother was crying.

Gently, Mrs Gavin reached out and ran her fingertips along April's cheek. "I'm so sorry," she whispered. "Oh, April, I'm so sorry." She brushed away her tears. "All I ever wanted was for you to be happy. It's still all I want. If you want to paint, than do it." She smiled, though tears were sliding down her face. "I still have the first picture you ever drew for me." She hugged April hard then. It was the first time she had been so affectionate and April clung to her, both of them crying.

"I want to go to art college, Dad." April tried to appease him. "It'll still be a college."

"You'll have to have some sort of a job, to support yourself," her father said grumpily, turning to her, still not convinced.

"I'll learn to type. I'll try any job once I can paint as well," April looked at him pleadingly. "Don't be angry, Dad, please. I'm sorry if I've let you down. I just can't bear for you to hate me."

The words cut him. "I could never hate you, you're my pride and joy." He came over to his wife and daughter. "I just want the best for you, April." His voice shook as he said, "If you want to paint and that's what makes you happy, well, it's your life, isn't it?" He tried to smile as he said, "Only one thing, though . . ."

April looked at him as he continued, "I'll kill you if you're not the best damn painter there is."

Chapter Twenty-One

Luke had driven for ages. Mrs Coleman began to relax. It was nice to be in a car, away from the house for a while, away from the monster that was her husband. Though what he'd do if he found out the car had been taken while he was working didn't bear thinking about. She hoped Luke would have the car back in the driveway before he got in at eight am. Luke seemed in good form, he had asked Davy where he wanted to go. Davy wanted to see the sea and so Luke had driven to Dún Laoghaire and along the coast road, smiling at his little brother's enthuasiam.

"Did Daddy let you have car?" he asked fearfully, when he had climbed inside.

"It's Luke's car," Luke had said firmly, and Davy had gleefully accepted it without question.

He was driving up the mountains now. The lights of Dublin winked and glowed orange and white in the distance. Luke stopped the car at the side of a sloping field and got out. "It's so quiet up here," he remarked as he began to walk around. Davy followed him and soon Luke was pointing out various landmarks. "The big dark patch in the middle, where no lights are, d'ya see that, Daves?"

Davy nodded.

"That's the Phoenix Park, one of the biggest parks in Europe. Those lights there," Luke pointed out a large area of lights, lit in a square, "that's the Central Mint, where all the money is made."

"Yeah?" Davy was impressed with that.

Mrs Coleman joined them. "I think we should be getting back," she said as she looked at her watch. "He'll be in around 8.00 am."

Luke ignored her. He walked over to the car, opened the door, leaned inside and shut the door again.

"What are you . . ." Mrs Coleman's voice faded away. She saw her son go to the back of the car and give it a gentle push. Very slowly the car began to roll down into the field, picking up speed as it went.

"Say 'bye' to daddy's car," Luke laughed, turning to both of them. There was a crash as the car slid down and into a tree where it eventually came to rest. Luke picked up a rock and hurled it at the car. "SEE YA," he yelled, shattering the horrified silence behind him.

Mrs Coleman sat on the ground, too sick to give out, too sick to cry, just numb. They had had it now . . . he would kill them.

To her surprise, Davy howled with laughter. "Daddy's car?" he confirmed with Luke who nodded. Davy laughed again. He too picked up a rock and, with all the strength in his small arm, hurled it after the car. "BYE, DADDY," he screamed. "BYE, BYE, DADDY."

He began to dance manically around and around, throwing whatever stones he could find after the car. Luke observed Davy for a minute and then went and sat down beside his mother.

Neither of them said anything for a while. Luke sifted gravel through his fingers, his mother looking on in despair as he did so.

"I feel good now," Luke said simply. "He feckin' taunts me with tha' bleedin' car – well, he can't any more. I just hate the bastard so much." He put his face in his hands and, in a broken voice, said, "I just can't take it any more, Ma. Please don't make me take it any more."

Mrs Coleman wrapped her arms around her son, his head on her breast. "I'm sorry, Luke," she whispered. "I did what I thought was best. I couldn't go anywhere, I had no money. I wanted you an' Davy to have a home an' warmth. I'm so sorry." She looked at her younger son, still shrieking with delight over the mangled remains of the car, and she knew that she had done them both a wrong. She had never discussed their father with them, never asked them how they felt; she had accepted her life in return for their home and food and clothes.

"I'm tired bein' afraid," Luke whispered. "I'm afraid all the time, Ma, what if he kills you or Daves? Don't make me go back."

"I've been saving," she said suddenly.

Luke looked up. "Yeah?"

"It's not much, only some of the money you gave me every week. I wanted to save up enough to get the three of us away from him an' still find a place near enough for your job." She shrugged, tears filling her eyes. "But then he began to take all your money an' I couldn't save any more. I've the book hidden up the chimney. I want you to have it."

Luke shook his head. "We'll stay together, Ma. Whatever you have, we'll manage."

"I only managed two hundred quid."

He took her by the shoulders. "We're goin' – you can't have Daves in tha' house any more."

"What can you get outa two hundred quid?" his mother asked in despair. "It's nothin', Luke."

"The plane to Manchester," Luke said excitedly as a thought struck him. "We can go to Manchester, Ma."

"What? Are you mad? Who do we know in Manchester?"

And so Luke told her.

It was time they took a chance.

April lay in the hotel bed, her hands under her head, staring at the ceiling. She was exhausted but she couldn't sleep. It was as if someone had waved a wand and made right all the years of hurt. Her parents were going to explain to Miss Allen, her form tutor, about the bullying. They said it would make Miss Allen and Mr Kavanagh understand better April's refusal to do detention. They did, however, expect her to apologise to Mr Kavanagh, and April had agreed. She didn't mind. She didn't have to prove anything to herself any more. She knew Kavanagh hadn't meant to sound like a bully, but everything had got confused in her head and she'd flipped.

April knew she would never allow herself to be bullied again.

Her parents said that they would ring the school in Cork and tell them about Mary. April didn't want them to do that, as she felt ashamed about being the victim of a bully, but they insisted. They said that Mary could be bullying someone else now and it was better that the teachers knew.

They also promised that in future they'd try and curtail their trips. They'd finish the stint in Germany and after that, providing her dad could find a position, they'd come to live in Dublin.

158

Her dad explained that he'd still have to go abroad from time to time, but April didn't mind. It was enough to know they cared. They even agreed to come to the football match tomorrow and see Luke play. That had nearly killed them.

They still didn't understand about Luke. April didn't think they ever would. She didn't understand herself, really.

She looked at her watch. It was nearly two am. She had tried to call Luke but there had been no answer. She wondered if she should try again. She didn't think he would mind her ringing him so late. She just couldn't wait until the morning to explain. She dialled his number and it began to ring.

"Yeah?" a narky, rough voice.

April bit her lip. God, should she say anything?

"Is that you, you fecker?" the voice was getting more irate. "You better not come home tonight, do you hear me?" The voice rose. "I swear, I'll kill ya. I swear I will."

April, her heart beating, gently put the phone down. She was positive she'd dialled the right number, but it couldn't have been. She decided it was a sign for her to leave things until the morning.

They walked all the way home, Luke giving Davy a piggy-back whilst Davy sang and cracked silly jokes. Luke grinned. "This is the way it should be always," he thought. He remembered that, when he was Davy's age, he had found out that not all Daddies hit their children. He remembered the rage he had felt that his da should keep hitting him, the rage that had stayed with him, the urge to lash back always in his mind. At least it stopped the terror, the terror that sometimes came in the night, the terror that stalked his dreams and made him cry out. The terror that showed in Davy's face every time Da got mentioned.

They had arrived home, though it wouldn't be their home for much longer. Luke unlocked the front door and the three went inside to the kitchen. Mrs Coleman quickly began to pack food and things they would need while Luke made his way upstairs to get a few of their clothes and put them in a suitcase. He froze at the last step; there was a noise coming from his parents' room, it was the sound of someone creeping about in the dark. Luke hid in the shadows, afraid it was a burglar, ready to jump on him if he came out. He watched in disbelief as the handle of the door slowly descended and a face peered out. A large, whiskey-red, moon-like face. What was his da doing home at this hour? He wasn't due off his shift till eight that morning.

Luke decided to bluff it out. He stepped into his father's line of vision, saying loudly, "DA?" in an effort to warn his mother. It worked; there was instant, wary silence from the kitchen. His father emerged, huge, large and snarling. "DON'T 'DA' ME," he roared. "WHERE WERE YOU ALL NIGHT? I RING AND SAY I'M COMIN' HOME AND NO ANSWER! WHERE THE HELL IS MY CAR?"

Luke tried to look surprised. "Is it not in the driveway? I didn't notice it had gone in the dark."

"You tryin' to kid me?" His father pressed his nose up against his son's. "Where is my car?" He was forcing Luke to the edge of the stairs. Luke tried to push against him, but couldn't. "Where is it?" his da said, the caressing voice far more menacing than any shouting.

"He doesn't know." Mrs Coleman had come to the

160

end of the stairway and stood looking up at her husband. She tried to keep the fear from her voice, it usually made him worse.

"Ah, my wife." Mr Coleman shoved Luke aside and began descending the stairs toward his wife. "And where were you till this hour?"

"Out."

"Where?"

Mrs Coleman took a deep breath. "In your precious car."

"No!" Luke yelled from the top of the stairs. "That's not true. Don't believe her, Da. I took the car." In two strides he was beside his mother. He was too late: a crashing blow sent her reeling toward the doorway. She lay there slumped like a rag doll.

Luke felt rage course through him. He launched himself on his da, and his father crashed around like a bull, but Luke was no match for him. He felt fists rain down on him before a final blow from his da sent him spinning into blackness.

Chapter Twenty-Two

Lunch in the Walshes was a noisy affair. On Bill's advice, Jack had refused to eat anything. "Might gimme cramp," he said mournfully.

Sarah began to make the most of eating a large cream cake in front of him. She licked her lips and, putting on a face of ecstasy, said, "Dee-licious!"

Jack manfully ignored her. He got up from the table and said that he was going to get his football kit. "The team bus is leavin' from Superquinn in half an hour, can't afford to be late." The match was being played in Tolka Park as large crowds were expected. The winning team would be featured on a special programme about amateur soccer in Ireland. Ballinteer were the hot favourites.

Sarah went to phone Frank to come on over.

Jack came bounding down the stairs, he jumped the last three and almost knocked Sarah down. "Sorry," he said grinning, "almost didn't see you there." Without waiting for a reply, he barged into the kitchen, yelled his goodbyes and went out, slamming the front door behind him.

"The noise he makes . . ." Mr Walsh grumbled as he began to clean off the table.

Sarah came back into the kitchen and gave a shriek that made her parents jump. She rushed over to her father and felt his forehead. "You all right, Da?" she asked in an anxious voice. "You sure you're in your right mind? You never ever help out with the kitchen."

Her mother began to laugh but her da didn't think it was funny. "Go and answer the door," he snapped. "The bell's ringing."

Still laughing, Sarah went into the hall. Seeing April through the frosted glass, she yelled, "It's April and her folks." She opened the door and grinned at the Gavins. "Come on in," she said. Glancing at April, she asked, "Things all right?"

April nodded. "Fine."

Sarah was bursting with curiosity, but hadn't the nerve to ask April anything in front of the Gavins.

April waited until her parents had gone into the kitchen before asking, "Have you heard from Luke today?"

Sarah shook her head. "No, why?"

"Aw, nothing." April had tried to call him again that morning but hadn't got an answer. She felt slightly concerned but decided not to say anything for the moment.

She followed Sarah into the kitchen. Her dad was talking and Mrs Walsh beckoned her over. "Everything all right?" she asked.

April nodded and, without thinking, leaned over and gave her a hug. "Thanks," she whispered. "And sorry for being such trouble."

Mrs Walsh was touched by the gesture. "Trouble," she scoffed. "What trouble?"

"Have to see this team in action," Mr Gavin was

saying. He turned to Mr Walsh, "We'll see what Jack is really made of."

"Jack's already headed off," Mr Walsh grinned.

He ushered them into the dining-room and took a bottle of whiskey from the sideboard. "Pre-match tipple?" he asked. "Help steady the oul' nerves."

Without waiting for an answer he poured Mr Gavin a generous whiskey and together they toasted the success of the team.

Frank arrived in at two o'clock, leather-clad and squeaky. He was introduced to the Gavins.

"How do you do?" Mr Gavin asked, trying not to gawk. The guy must carry the weight of ten dead animals on his shoulders, he thought.

"Cool, I'm cool, Doc," Frank drawled. He swaggered out into the hallway looking for Sarah.

April noticed disbelieving looks pass between her parents. Pity they hadn't met Frank before they met Luke, she thought. At least Luke looked normal.

Frank allowed Sarah to simper over him. He smiled benignly down at her and played the part of the conquering hero. He refused her offer of tea; instead, gazing at a huge watch on his wrist, he said, "Come on, hon, let's hit the road."

"Just a sec." Sarah ran into the hall and appeared back with the banner April had made. "I thought it would be great to go to the match with this flying behind us on the bike," she announced. "There's a great breeze out today."

Frank gazed at her in disbelief. "It would overturn the bike, hon," he explained.

"If you drive nice an' slow, we won't get hurt."

"Yeah, but what about the bike? What if somethin'

164

happens to me bike?" Frank looked horrified as he shook his head. "No way, babe. No can do."

Mr Gavin let out a shout of laughter which he tried to cover up.

"You and your flippin' bike," Sarah fumed, mortified. "It's borin', that's what it is – borin'."

Frank shrugged, unperturbed. "I think this match is borin' – don't mean I wanna wreck it."

This made no sense to anyone except the infatuated Sarah. She beamed at his irrefutable logic, handed the flag to April and waltzed out the door with him.

"I wish I could calm her down like that," Mrs Walsh remarked as she watched her daughter drive off with the Plank. "Where on earth did she find him?"

The Gavins were wondering the same thing.

"Suppose we better be makin' a move." Mr Walsh slugged back his remaining whiskey, got up from his seat and went to get everyone's coats. April wrapped her blue-and-white scarf around her neck and carried the banner out to the car.

Mrs Walsh was elected to drive.

April turned to her parents as they sat in the back with her and said, "I know you'll love the match, I just know it!" Pressing their hands in her own, she smiled. "Thanks for coming, anyhow."

They smiled back, glad to have made her happy in this one thing at least.

Luke awoke to a gentle tugging on his arm. God, he felt so awful.

He had a pain deep in his ribs, a hammering in his head.

"Luke, Luke," the voice said. "Daddy's gone now."

Then, on the verge of a sob, "Please, Luke, wake up. I can't wake Mammy."

Luke closed his eyes, but the voice kept tugging him awake again. Slowly the fog cleared. His eyes blinked beneath heavy lids and struggled to open. He held up an arm as if to block out the memory of last night. His father had kept hitting him every time he moved.

"Please, Luke. Help Mammy."

"What . . ." Mr Walsh was gazing out his window. He ordered his wife to stop the car. "Is that the team bus?"

When she nodded, he said, "Why on earth hasn't it left yet? They were due to leave at 1.30. It's 2.15 now." He decided to go over and find out what was wrong.

He arrived back to the car a few minutes later. "They're waiting on Coleman." He gazed at April as if it was her fault. When she said nothing, he continued, "I told them to go on. I said we'd pick Luke up and get him there. Of all the bloody days he decides to be late!"

"I rang earlier and there was no answer from his place," April said. "He's left, I know he has. He wouldn't let the team down."

Mr Walsh gave a sigh of exasperation. "He's done it before, this won't be the first time. That lad suits himself."

"He's not like that," April snapped back. Her mother gave her a dig in the ribs and told her to stay quiet. April ignored her.

"He isn't like that," she muttered, hoping that they could all hear.

"Just cool it," Mrs Walsh said placidly from the driver's seat. She turned to her husband. "You'd better tell me where Luke lives."

"It's not far," he said. "Just down the road and to the left."

He vowed to himself that, when he got his hands on the kid, he'd give him a piece of his mind.

Luke jumped at the sound of the doorbell. He gazed fearfully out the window and saw April standing on the doorstep. His heart began to hammer, beads of sweat broke out on his forehead. He couldn't possibly let April see him like this. He had to get rid of her before the doctor came.

"Daves," he whispered. "There's a girl at the door, she's lookin' for me – tell her I'm not here."

Davy whimpered. He was holding on to his mother's hand and wouldn't leave her. Luke dragged him up and shoved him toward the door. "Tell her I'm gone out," he whispered again.

Davy nodded and opened the door.

April smiled at him. "Hi, Davy," she said brightly. "You are Davy, aren't you?"

Davy nodded dumbly, his eyes fixed on the girl.

"Is Luke here? I'm looking for him."

Davy shook his head. "No, he's out."

"Is he gone to the match?" April asked. She saw Davy's eyes grow wide in confusion.

"He's out," Davy reiterated.

"Is your mammy there?" April tried again. "I just want to see if she knows where your brother is?" She looked in horror as the little boy in front of her began to sob.

"What's the matter?" April asked. She hadn't a clue what to do, she didn't know much about kids. "Have you a pain?"

167

Davy shook his head. "Mammy's sick."

"Is your daddy there, then?" April was floundering. She wished she hadn't insisted on going to the door. The child began to howl.

Behind her she heard Mrs Walsh coming up the path. "What's the problem?"

April shrugged. "He just started to cry – I don't know why . . ."

Mrs Walsh put her arms around Davy. "Now, now," she soothed him. "What's the matter, honey? Are you on your own?"

Davy shook with sobs. "Mammy sick, Mammy sick," he whimpered.

Mrs Walsh looked at April. "I'll just go and see what the story is," she whispered. "I hope they haven't left him on his own with a sick mother."

Before she got into the hall, Luke appeared in the kitchen doorway. He stayed in the shadow of the door frame.

April gasped. "Luke, what's wrong? The flipping team bus is waiting for you. Why on earth aren't you there?"

"I'm not going," Luke stated, arms folded. "Just go – don't come any nearer."

April shook her head. "I don't believe you – Luke?"

He turned from her. "Just get out," he said savagely.

"I will not," Mrs Walsh surprised the two of them with her firmness. She indicated Davy. "This brother of yours is terribly upset – what's wrong with him?"

"I'll take care of him," Luke replied. "Come on over, Daves."

Davy buried his head further into Mrs Walsh's skirt. "Don't want to stay here – Mammy sick."

"Davy," Luke said sharply, an edge of panic in his voice.

Davy wouldn't budge.

"Where is your mother?" Mrs Walsh asked. "Are you looking after her?"

Luke nodded. "Me, eh, da, he's gone ta get the doctor. I'm lookin' after Davy."

"My dad's a doctor," April said. "He'll have a look at your mum. You go to the match, Luke, and I'll take care of Davy – how's that?"

"NO!" Luke made them jump. He bit his lip. "It's OK," he said. "We can manage."

"It makes sense," April pleaded with him. "Please, Luke, forget about last night. Let my dad look at her."

Luke gulped. His head hurt. "Please, just go," he said wearily.

Mrs Walsh shrugged. She gave Luke a withering look. "All right, but you're letting the whole team down."

Davy began to scream as he saw them leave. He grabbed hold of Mrs Walsh's legs and begged her not to go.

"What's going on?" Mrs Walsh demanded as she scooped the little boy up in her arms. "You'd better tell me, 'cause I'm not leaving the child in this state."

Luke rubbed his hands over his face; things were falling apart. He made no protest as Mrs Walsh barged past him into the kitchen.

Ballinteer lined out against Maynooth Celtic. Sarah groaned as she saw them. "Jack is playin' midfield," she exclaimed. "He's rubbish in that position. Luke should be there. I wonder where Bill has him?" She searched the eleven for Luke. "The fecker isn't playin'. He's let them down again." She turned to Frank. "Oh, Frank, you'd better start prayin'."

Frank grinned. He just wanted it to lash rain and the match to be called off – now that would suit him fine.

"I can't see April anywhere, either," Sarah was scanning the crowd. "I thought she'd be waving the banner for them."

Frank shoved another few peanuts into his mouth. He wished the wind would get a bit stronger, maybe then it might be too stormy to play.

He groaned as the ref blew the whistle for the start of the match.

Mr Walsh's car arrived at the admissions department of the hospital and April jumped out. "Want me to come with you?" Mr Walsh asked her.

"No, thanks all the same," April gazed at the huge hospital building. "I'll just see what the news is." Turning once again to Mr Walsh, she said, "You might as well go and see what's left of the match – no point in us all missing it."

Mr Walsh was hoping someone would say that. It was killing him missing Jack play in the cup-final. Still, he felt, maybe he should go home to his wife and see how that little brother of Luke's was doing. Glumly, he shook his head – one never knew what went on behind closed doors. He had always thought that Mr Coleman was a nice enough bloke. He started the car and waved goodbye to April. One never knew.

April followed the signs to the casualty department. Her heart was hammering,. She hadn't a clue what she was going to do when she found Luke, but she knew that she just had to see him. Her stomach still felt queasy every time she thought of his mother lying on the floor in the kitchen. Her body had been twisted, her face bruised and bloody. The kitchen had been destroyed. Davy had pointed to the broken cups and plates. "Daddy," he had nodded. "He hurt Mammy, then . . ." his voice trailed off. Luke had said nothing, he just stood staring at them.

April had run outside to the car, screaming for her father. He had examined Luke's mother and immediately ordered an ambulance.

"I did ring for a doctor," Luke muttered.

"You'd better go in for a check-up, too," Mr Gavin had put his hands on the boy's shoulders and sat him down. "You've a few nasty cuts there." Then, turning to Davy, he asked gently, "Did Daddy hit you?"

Davy shook his head. "Luke showed me this place to hide. Daddy never finds me." He went to Luke and took his hand. Luke gave it a brief squeeze.

The ambulance took Mr Gavin, Luke and his mother to the hospital. Mrs Walsh had packed a few clothes for Mrs Coleman and handed the case to April to take to the hospital. "Dan'll drive you in. Your mother and I will bring Davy back to our place. Tell Luke to come back there too when he's finished."

April, case in hand, arrived at casualty admissions. The place was bedlam, the nurses on the desk very busy. It took about five minutes before April could ask the nurse if she knew where Mrs Coleman and her son Luke had gone.

The nurse looked at her chart. "They came in an ambulance about twenty minutes ago?"

April nodded. "About that, I suppose."

"Dr Gavin took the woman to the operating theatre. She'll be a while. Is that her case?"

April nodded and handed it over. "We'll get it to her." The nurse turned to another patient.

"Her son?" April prompted. "She came in with her son?"

The nurse looked again. "Oh, he was taken for observation. He's in one of the cubicles over there." She waved to her left.

April didn't know what to do. Should she go over and look for Luke? She hadn't a clue what to say to him but she didn't want to leave him on his own. Making up her mind, she strode purposefully over to the cubicles.

"Luke?" she called tentatively.

There was no answer.

April began to look into each little room. She was lucky and found him in the second one she tried. He was lying on a makeshift bed, staring at the ceiling.

"Luke?"

His head turned briefly towards her. April was reminded of the night they first met, when he had dismissed her with his glance.

"How are you feeling?"

He shrugged.

"My dad's with your mother – he'll see she's fine."

"Yeah." He wished she'd go away.

"Luke?"

He stared at her then. "Don't say it, April. Don't say you're sorry – just don't."

April sat down beside the bed. "I wasn't going to . . . I just wanted to know why you never said anything – you could have told me, you know."

"Aw, sure, yeah," Luke sneered. "By the way, April,

me da beats the shite outa me an' me ma. Yeah, good one."

"I didn't mean it like that," April knew this was coming out all wrong – she hadn't got a good bedside manner at all. "I just meant that, like, I told you things and you could have told me stuff back."

Luke raised himself up on his elbow. "Oh, yeah, you told me loadsa stuff. Like how you didn't want to let your parents down, like how you always stood up for yourself – nothin' about how bloody scared you were of things. Gimme a break, April." Luke collapsed back on to the bed and turned his head away from her.

April bit her lip. "I was too ashamed, too embarrassed."

"How the hell do ya think I feel now?" Luke said. "The one girl I really like, to see me like this. How could I have told you, April?"

April shrugged. "I dunno."

Luke shook his head. "I wanted to forget about it all when I was with you. If you knew, I reckoned it would wreck things. I was someone different when I was with you." He stopped and closed his eyes. He felt dizzy. Then April's arms were around him, her hair falling across his face.

"I was someone different when I was with you, too," she whispered. "You made me feel I could do anything." She gave a shaky sigh. "I'm so sorry about last night and the way I treated you. I rang this morning to say that, but there was no answer."

Luke could feel her tears mingling with his. Everything suddenly made sense, everything, and the fact that things made sense made him cry all the more.

"Sarah!"

Sarah turned to find her dad trying to push his way past some spectators in an effort to reach her. He arrived at her side eventually, giving a curt nod to Frank.

"Where have you been sittin'?" Sarah asked. "I've been lookin' all over the ground for you."

"Just got here," Mr Walsh glanced sharply at Frank. He didn't know how much to say in front of him. Still, he figured his daughter would tell him, anyhow. "We went to pick up Luke and, well, there had been a bit of an accident – he's at the hospital."

Sarah looked shocked. "Serious?"

"Serious enough. His mother's in bad shape, Luke's not too bad. His little brother is at our house."

"What happened? Oh, God, I feel so guilty. I've been cursin' Luke the whole match long, haven't I, Frank?"

Frank looked surprised. He had switched off, he hadn't listened to a word she had said since the game started. "Oh, yeah, yeah," he muttered, glancing at his watch, wondering how much more he'd have to endure.

"What happened?" Sarah asked again.

Mr Walsh felt sickened as he said, "Luke's da – he, well, he beat them."

Sarah gasped and even Frank looked shocked.

Mr Walsh tapped the side of his nose. "That's just between us, all right?"

"Yeah," Sarah nodded. "Poor Luke."

"So," Mr Walsh tried to change the subject, "how's the match going?" He began to scan the pitch for Jack. Midfield, Bill had him in midfield, he couldn't believe it! What a bad decision. "What's the score?" he asked.

Sarah groaned. "Two-nil to Maynooth. Our lads haven't

a hope at this stage." She offered her father a sweet. "Luke should be out there – he'd have made such a difference. For one thing, they wouldn't be able to walk up the pitch with balls like that. YEZ ARE WOEFUL!" She screamed at Jack as he ran past, vainly trying to stop their winger from getting a cross in.

Frank winced inwardly, God, Sarah was so loud.

The winger made a beautiful cross on to the six-yard line.

The Maynooth striker, unmarked, powerfully headed the ball.

A third goal went in.

There were disappointed groans from Ballinteer supporters.

Bill was yelling at his team from the bench.

The ref blew for full time.

Frank heaved a sigh of relief and prepared to go home.

"I'll catch up with you," Mr Walsh said to Sarah. "I just want to go over and explain Luke's absence to Bill. He can tell the team in the dressing-room. I don't want the lad getting blamed for something he couldn't help."

Sarah sighed. "Yeah, right. Janey, what a terrible match. I suppose we'd better hang on like good sports and watch Maynooth collect the cup."

Frank could have strangled her. Instead he shrugged. "Yeah, righ'."

Luke had been declared all right by a student doctor. "A few bruised ribs, nothing broken. Headache is probably tension, no concussion; you're a lucky lad." He handed Luke some painkillers, nodded curtly to April and marched out of the room.

Luke climbed down from the bed and gave a half grin. "I've never been called lucky before," he joked. He stared at April as he took her hand in his. "Thanks."

April hugged him gently, mindful of his ribs. "Come on, let's see if we can find out anything about your mum." She led him from the cubicle.

"April, Luke?"

April turned at the sound of her father's voice. He advanced toward them. "How are you, son?" he asked.

Luke shrugged. "All righ'. How's me ma?"

Mr Gavin smiled. "She'll be all right, eventually. She has some bad internal injuries, but she'll recover. I know the doctor who operated, he's a good man."

Luke nodded. He held out his hand. "Thank you, I appreciate it."

Mr Gavin grasped his hand hard. "I guess I owe you thanks as well. We started on the wrong foot. Only for you, my daughter informs me, things would never have been sorted out last night."

Luke shrugged. "Can I see me ma?"

"Not for the moment, she's still sleepy. Your best bet is to get some rest."

"Mrs Walsh says to come to their house," April said. "I suppose you won't be going back to your place."

"Oh, by the way," Mr Gavin pulled a small brown book wrapped in plastic from his pocket. "We found this on your mother – I think it's a savings book."

Luke took it. "We were leavin' this mornin'." He gave a rueful laugh. "I got a trial for Man United an' I was goin' to ring them to fix a date. They'd fly me an' another person over, so all we had to pay for was Davy." He sighed. "We were goin' to take a chance."

April smiled. "You still can – go for the trial while your mother's in here. Mrs Walsh will take care of Davy. I think she's adopted him at this stage, anyhow."

Luke shrugged. "Aw, I dunno."

"Well, I do," April stared hard at him. "God, Luke, you're a brilliant footballer, they'll be mad not to book you."

Luke laughed. "They don't 'book' you," he grinned affectionately at April. "They sign you. Anyhow, do you even know who United are?"

"Yeah, a football team."

"The best flippin' team in England – janey, they've Cole, Giggs and Roy flippin' Keane playin' for them."

"Yeah, and if you go, they'll have Luke flippin' Coleman as well." She gave him a push. "Go on, ring them – have you still got their card?"

"At home," Luke replied glumly. Then, grinning, he said, "But I betcha Bill has the number – janey, it'll make his bleedin' year, one of his lads gettin' a try-out for United."

"Well, find Bill, so."

"You're mad, April Gavin."

"I'll be a lot madder if you don't give it a shot," April said severely.

Mr Gavin smiled at the two of them. "And you said *I* was a bossy you-know-what," he joked.

Luke looked slightly ashamed for a second but, upon seeing Mr Gavin smile, he smiled back. "At least I know where she gets it from," he slagged.

"Well, are you going for the – the yoke, whatever you call it?" April demanded.

"The trial," Luke said. "It's a trial."

"Well, are you going?"

"I'd be bleedin' afraid not to," Luke joked.

"Good," April grinned up at him and took his hand in hers and squeezed it.

Together they walked on and left Mr Gavin standing there.

April had a look about her today, her father couldn't place it. Then it came to him. She was walking with her head in the air, looking the world in the eye. Confidence, that was it. She looked confident and . . . and happy, he thought.

Chapter Twenty-Three

April sat in her usual seat in Mr Kavanagh's class. She grinned around at her classmates, saying, "I heard there was no excitement in biology since I left, so here I am, back again." There was rowdy laughter and a few claps of welcome.

"He's comin'! He's comin'!" The warning flew around the room and there was silence as Mr Kavanagh walked in. He marched to the top of the room and whirled around suddenly. This was his usual method of starting a lesson. Anyone caught whispering, nudging or "foostering" was given a hard time for the rest of the period. His eyes roamed the room. He found nothing amiss.

Clearing his throat, he began to speak. "No doubt the more intelligent life forms here have noticed that Ms April Gavin is again among us. For those of you who haven't been quick enough to spot this, there she is." He waved his arm in April's general direction. No one moved. No one looked at her. They knew better. "Ms Gavin and I have reached an understanding." He smiled suddenly and looked at April. "Isn't that right?"

April nodded, blushing furiously. Mr Kavanagh had been very supportive when he heard her story. He said that he hadn't meant to sound as if he was bullying her;

all he was doing was teaching in the only way he knew how, by instilling discipline and respect for the subject into his students. He insisted that she sit the test again but he told her not to worry about the detention. Then he had apologised for criticising her in front of everybody.

April felt she had to acknowledge his kindness in some way. To everyone's surprise, including her own, she stood up. "I'd just like to say," she began haltingly, "that there were reasons why I reacted the way I did when I stated that I wouldn't do detention." She gulped, all eyes were upon her and she hated it. "I explained to Kav, eh, Mr Kavanagh and he's been dead nice about it."

Mr Kavanagh bowed graciously amid the "feck off's" of amazement issuing from his students.

April shrugged. "Thanks for letting me back in."

There was silence as she sat down.

"Now, see how great I am," Kavanagh boomed. He pointed his finger at the rest of the class. "I'm warning the rest of you – don't mess with me."

He turned to write on the board.

"You're some operator," the fella beside April whispered in admiration. "He kicks you out of class and then he's all over you." He grinned. "Betcha blackmailed him – some sleazy double life he's leadin' an' you found out."

April giggled. "Yeah," she grinned. "Got it in one." She lowered her voice and tried to say menacingly, "No one, not even Kavanagh, crosses me."

Chapter Twenty-Four

They had all come to the airport to see him off, the Walshes, Davy and most important of all, April.

Luke grinned. The Walshes had been so good, letting him and Davy stay at their place until Luke's trial came up. Luke had continued to work for Jimmy and he had given Mrs Walsh his wages. She had initially refused the money but, when she had seen the look of hurt on his face, she had relented. "It's for Daves and me ma. To help pay for them when me ma gets out," he explained seriously. "I'll be a week over there – me ma will be with you for a few days, I can't let her think she's sponging off you. I know it's not much, but I'll give you more when I get it."

Mrs Walsh wondered how she had ever disliked Luke. "Your mother can stay as long as she likes," she replied, pocketing the money. "Don't worry about paying us back – God knows, we can afford it."

Luke bit his lip and said nothing. He didn't know what he would do if this trial fell through. Still, Bill seemed to think that he'd have no problem getting a place on an Irish soccer team.

Luke looked around for Bill who had offered to go to the trial with him. He was acting as his manager, coach, advisor. Bill was thrilled with his protégé's decision.

"You won't regret this," he kept saying as he clapped Luke on the back. He had almost forgiven him for missing the cup-final.

Luke's father hadn't contacted him at all. Luke had written a note telling him that they were applying for a barring order and also that social workers had been contacted. Mr Walsh had placed it on the kitchen table when he had gone to pick up Luke and Davy's things.

"Oy, Coleman!"

Everyone jumped at the sound of the loud brash voice. Luke grinned. "Jimmy, how's it goin'?"

April started. This was the "Jimmy" she had heard so much about – he wasn't at all like she'd pictured.

Jimmy walked into the middle of the little gathering and took Luke by the hand. He faced everyone. "I came to wish you luck," he said. "In a way I hope you don't get it, cause I'll be bleedin' stuck with a dumb numbskull as a co-driver."

Luke laughed. Jimmy, in an effort to win back his wife, had agreed to give his son a part-time job working with him while Luke was going for his trial. The understanding was that, if Luke left, there was a job for Jimmy junior on the truck. Jimmy was in bits at the possibility.

"This is me driver, Jim," Luke introduced Jimmy to everyone.

Jimmy leered at Sarah. "This the gorgeous April I've heard so much about?" he asked lustfully.

"Naw, this is," Luke took April's hand in his. Jimmy nodded briefly at April and switched his attention back to Sarah.

Mr Walsh glared at him.

Jack thought it was hilarious. "Sugar daddy," he whispered in Sarah's ear as he passed her.

"Get lost," Sarah hissed. She began to tell Jimmy all about her boyfriend.

Mrs Walsh decided that sometimes the Plank came in useful after all.

It was time to go. Bill was yanking his arm. Luke said "goodbye" to everyone and, turning to April, he kissed her long and hard. There was no need to say anything.

"Will you come on," Bill laughed. "Feck's sake, you'll have no energy for football after that."

Everyone laughed.

"Call me?" April said tearfully. She couldn't bear to let go of his hand.

"I'll call you tonight," Luke promised. He wiped her tears gently away with his thumb. "Don't," he whispered as he cupped her face in his hand. "I'll always be around for you."

"Promise?"

"Yeah." He kissed her softly and said, "I'll be seein' you."

"Yeah – see you," April reluctantly let his hand go and watched him walk away.

"Good luck," she called.

He turned back and raised his hand in acknowledgement.

Extract from the *Evening Herald*

NEW IRISH PLAYER SIGNS FOR UNITED

It has been confirmed by Manchester United boss, Alex Ferguson, that he has signed young Irish amateur league player, Luke Coleman (19).

Ferguson is reportedly delighted with the youngster. "He's confident on the ball, fearless, skilful and will hopefully be playing first team football in the near future."

Coleman has been drafted into the decimated United side at just the right time. With more players being added to their nightmare injury list each week, Coleman will have ample opportunity to prove himself.

Luke Coleman, from Ballinteer in Dublin, has only ever played with amateur league team Ballinteer United. He has expressed no fears about his ability to play at the top levels.

With the brash confidence and fearlessness of youth, Coleman states, "I have waited all my life for this. I know I can do it."